VICTORIES

Spirit was scared and confused, but she kept trying to do the right thing, not the easy thing.

Even when it looked like the right thing would just get her killed.

She was scared, but she'd faced the Demon Lord of Hell, even though she'd been so terrified she could hardly stand up. Because it was the right thing to do. And this was an even bigger fight, and she didn't think she was the right person for it—that any of them were—and it would even look like being smart to try to get to Addie's trustees for help instead of trying to do this themselves. Nobody would blame her if she said she'd changed her mind.

But it would be wrong. This is our fight, and I have to stop telling myself nobody expects me to be a hero. It doesn't matter if I don't think I'm a hero, either. I'm going to do everything I can, no matter what it is.

"Do you hear me?" she shouted. "I don't care what you do! I'm not giving up! I may not be Oakhurst's definition of a winner, but I'm not what you're trying to say I am! I won't give up! I won't!"

TOR TEEN BOOKS BY
MERCEDES LACKEY AND ROSEMARY EDGHILL

Mercedes Lackey and Rosemary Edghill

Shadow Grail 4

VICTORIES

TOR®
TEEN

A Tom Doherty Associates Book

New York

This is a work of fiction. All of the characters, organizations, and events portrayed in this novel are either products of the authors' imaginations or are used fictitiously.

SHADOW GRAIL #4: VICTORIES

A Tor Teen Book
Published by Tom Doherty Associates, LLC
175 Fifth Avenue
New York, NY 10010

www.tor-forge.com

Tor® is a registered trademark of Tom Doherty Associates, LLC.

Library of Congress Cataloging-in-Publication Data

Lackey, Mercedes, author.
   Victories / Mercedes Lackey and Rosemary Edghill.
      p. cm. — (Shadow Grail ; 4)
   "A Tom Doherty Associates book."
   ISBN 978-0-7653-2826-7 (hardcover)
   ISBN 978-0-7653-1764-3 (trade paperback)
   ISBN 978-1-4668-4321-9 (e-book)
   1. Magic—Fiction.   2. Supernatural—Fiction.   3. Mordred
(Legendary character)—Fiction.   4. Boarding schools—Fiction.
5. Schools—Fiction.   I. Edghill, Rosemary, author.   II. Title.
   PZ7.L13543Vi 2014
   [Fic]—dc23

                                                    2013025956

Tor Teen books may be purchased for educational, business, or promotional use. For information on bulk purchases, please contact Macmillan Corporate and Premium Sales Department at 1-800-221-7945, extension 5442, or write specialmarkets@macmillan.com.

First Edition: April 2014

Printed in the United States of America

0   9   8   7   6   5   4   3   2   1

To Vanessa Jayne Cartwright
Mysteriously.

Shadow Grail 4

VICTORIES

ONE

The black van bumped along the road, jarring Spirit's spine with every lurch. Burke was at the wheel, driving toward a destination that wasn't even a point on a map. The instructions he was following were a list of distances and landmarks: they'd crossed from Montana into North Dakota hours ago, but for all any of the four of them knew, their destination might be the middle of the Atlantic Ocean.

It's Saturday morning, Spirit thought wearily, feeling drunk from lack of sleep, as she gazed out the side window at the unchanging vista of fields and trees and distant mountains. It was spring—almost April—but the landscape looked barren to her. It was nothing like the place she'd grown up. Her life was nothing like the one she'd had the last time she'd looked out a car window counting the weeks to summer.

Her life? It was an unreal nightmare, the stuff of B movies.

Except it was happening, and it was almost uniformly horrible.

A year ago, Saturday had been a day to hang out with friends, to tease her younger sister, to make elaborate kitchen experiments with Dad or go on adventures with Mom. But that was before the— *Don't call it an accident now, call it what it was. Murder.* Murder. Before the Shadow Knights murdered her family. Before everything changed.

Six months ago, she'd just been told she was going to go to a place called Oakhurst because there was nowhere else for her to go with all her family dead. From the beginning, Spirit had known there was something *wrong* with Oakhurst. *Yeah, maybe the fact that someone was trying to kill us off might have been the hint.* But that was simplifying things; the facade that Oakhurst had kept up was too good. The whole horrible scope of how badly things were wrong had taken a while to figure out. In fact, it hadn't been until a week ago that she really understood, when she'd gotten the last clues to put it all together.

She'd been told when she arrived that Oakhurst wasn't a normal orphanage, but a school for magicians. Which had been unsettling, and scary, but could have been kind of cool if the people in charge hadn't been pitting every student against every other student, in a kind of just-sub-lethal Hunger Games.

But then she found out that if you had magic, Oakhurst's headmaster tracked you down and killed your family, and then made it look as if they'd wanted you to be sent there.

Loch's father had died in a hotel fire, Muirin's in an automobile accident, Addie's in a plane crash, Burke's in a home invasion. Hers, in another car crash. The method didn't matter. Only the results. That you got sent to Oakhurst, where the headmaster could decide if you were worth the effort of teaching. Because if he decided you weren't—well, the Hunger Games stopped being *sub*-lethal.

And I thought all along he'd made a mistake about me, that I didn't have magic. But he hadn't. She looked down at her hands. There was still a pale mark on the left one where her school ring had been. The stone changed color when it recognized your magic, and hers never had.

Until last night.

And now I know I'm a Spirit Mage, and I know my School of Magic is the School of Spirit, but that's all I know. They taught four Schools of Magic at Oakhurst. Dr. Ambrosius made everyone forget there were five.

She didn't know why, but considering everything else, it almost didn't matter. Dr. Ambrosius wanted to bring everyone with magic to Oakhurst so he could either recruit them— or kill them. Because in his world, there were only flunkies and enemies, and he wasn't just a magician. And his real name wasn't Ambrosius.

His real name was Mordred. *The* Mordred. Centuries ago, he'd lost a war for a kingdom. His enemies had locked him in a prison they'd hoped would last forever—but just in case it didn't, his jailers had cast a second spell, binding all of them to be reborn over and over until the threat was ended forever. To become *Reincarnates,* unaware of who they'd been until Merlin—or Mordred—awakened their memories.

Merlin. Mordred. Arthur. Guinevere. Names out of a storybook until Spirit and her friends discovered it wasn't a story—it was something they were all living. Because Dr. Ambrosius was Mordred, and once he'd escaped his prison, he gathered an army of Shadow Knights to serve him, and spent decades hunting the Grail Knights who were the only challengers to his power.

He built Oakhurst as the means to do that. He eliminated every magician who wouldn't serve him before they could even begin to threaten him. And who would ever have believed he was doing anything like that, when no one in the outside world had so much as a *clue* that magic was real?

A day ago, Spirit finally found a way for the five of them to escape from Oakhurst. If escape had been their only goal, there wouldn't have been any point—but escape was only the beginning of what they were going to have to do.

Save the world. Why is it that's always what it turns out to be?

Maybe because when it was *things* like Mordred you were up against, they weren't going to settle for anything less than the world.

It was Muirin who'd infiltrated the Shadow Knights to discover Mordred planned to trigger a nuclear apocalypse to create a world where Magic, not Science, ruled. They'd fled knowing they were the only ones who had a chance to stop it. A mysterious ally Spirit knew only as QUERCUS had given them a place to go.

But escape had come at far too high a price.

The van hit another pothole, and Spirit groaned faintly.

"Sorry," Burke said, glancing at her apologetically. "You okay?"

"Thinking about Muirin," she said. She closed her eyes hard, willing herself not to cry. It wouldn't do any good. Muirin would still be dead.

Muirin clung to Doc Mac's arm as the dancers at the Spring Fling swirled around them, oblivious. She looked greenish-pale, and the dark smudges under her eyes had nothing to do with makeup. Spirit saw her lurch and stagger, and only Doc Mac's grip on her arm kept her from falling.

"Muirin!" Spirit cried.

She pushed through the crowd, shoving people out of her way as she headed for Muirin. She was about halfway there when Muirin saw her. She brought her hand up and made a throwing motion. The car keys came flying through the air, and Spirit snatched them without thought. Muirin silently mouthed one word:

"Run."

Not everyone with magic was a Reincarnate, but Spirit had been sure about Muirin. Anastus Ovcharenko—Shadow Knight and Mordred's pet assassin—had called Muirin and Madison Lane-Rider "sisters"—and that made Madison Lane-Rider Queen Morgause and Muirin Queen Morgaine. Madison was a Shadow Knight, and Muirin had played a long double game, pretending she wanted to join them while remaining loyal to her friends. Maybe Murr-cat had been tempted to swap sides—maybe she'd even come close, and who could have blamed her? The other side had . . . everything. What did her friends have? But Muirin had stuck with them. Without Muirin's last-minute warning—without her *help*—Mordred would have gotten all five of them.

Instead of only one of them.

Burke reached out a hand and closed it over hers. "They will pay for that. I swear it," he said.

"Do you think—?" she said, hating herself for hoping. She'd seen Muirin fall, shot by Anastus Ovcharenko—Prince Agravaine. But maybe. . . .

"No," Burke said quietly. "They'd never have trusted her after she helped us. He shot to kill."

I won't cry, Spirit told herself desperately, but despite her best efforts, a tear slid down her cheek.

"It's no sin to grieve," Burke said gently.

"We don't have time," Spirit answered angrily. "Mordred's going to nuke the world back to the Stone Age!"

"We have time to mourn for our friend. Mordred moves on Beltane," Burke said. "That's May first. It's only the end of March now."

"Great," Spirit said, rubbing her eyes, her throat and heart aching. "Six weeks to save the world."

Silence hung between them, stretching the tension to the

breaking point. "I hope this Internet buddy of yours can help," Burke finally said, awkwardly changing the subject.

She took the change of subject gratefully, thankful for his kindness. "Me, too," Spirit answered somberly.

"Are we there yet?" Loch asked, sitting up and leaning forward between the seats. He and Addie were riding in the back. Spirit could have ridden in back too, and maybe even gotten some sleep—QUERCUS had left the van for them, along with the directions to reach their destination—but she'd wanted to be with Burke.

"Don't make me pull this getaway car over," Burke said lightly, and despite everything, Spirit smiled.

She'd never had a boyfriend before. She'd never expected to find one at Oakhurst. After her family died, she'd just wanted to shut out the world, and never care about anyone again. But Burke had loved her—as simply and as uncomplicatedly as breathing—from almost the moment he'd first seen her. When she'd realized she was in love with him too, it was too late to turn back and pretend she wasn't. It was the most wonderful thing in her life. It was the most terrible thing too, because she'd known they were all in danger before the first time Burke had kissed her, and the thought she could lose him the way she'd lost her family was terrifying.

To lose anyone else, really, and she'd already lost Muirin, and she knew it hadn't really sunk in yet, but it already hurt so much she just wanted to scream until she couldn't scream any more.

"Are we going to be awake now?" Addie asked grumpily, sitting up next to Loch. She glanced out the windshield. "Ugh. It looks the same as it did the last time I looked. Where are we going?"

"I don't know, but we're making good time," Burke joked.

They were all concentrating on trivial stuff, or trying to, and Spirit didn't blame them. Easier not to talk about the danger, the deaths, the fact they weren't safe, even now. "Wherever it is, we should be there in a couple of hours, tops," Spirit said, waving the sheaf of directions. "According to this, anyway."

"I hope wherever it is it involves thick walls and strong doors," Loch said. "And maybe landmines. Because I'm pretty sure Breakthrough isn't going to stop chasing us."

"Not if Mordred wants them to," Addie said, shuddering. "I wouldn't want to be the one he got mad at."

"Except you totally are," Loch pointed out. "We all are."

"Yeah," Burke said reasonably. "But at least we can run for our lives. I wouldn't want to be one of his henchmen."

"I don't think *Mark* wants to be one of his henchmen right now, either," Addie said.

"Too bad," Spirit said venomously. "He had the same choice everyone else got, and he chose Mordred."

"Yeah, cake or death, great choice," Loch said. "I'm not excusing him—his so-called 'security people' killed our families, as I'm sure we all remember—but he probably never expected the Evil Overlord's plan to be starting a nuclear war just so he didn't have to deal with the real world."

"It doesn't make *sense*," Addie said plaintively. "He's a magician—we've all seen how much power he has. Mordred could probably have taken over a country and made himself king years ago. There are thousands of places where if you walked in and said you could cure disease and make the crops grow and could prove it, they'd fall all over themselves to hand you the keys to the kingdom."

"So to speak," Loch said, with a wry smile. "Stubborn and stupid is a bad combination, but he's just like a lot of CEOs my father dealt with. And remember—Mordred isn't a Reincarnate."

Suddenly, some of this made a twisted sort of sense to Spirit. Mordred had been Mordred for centuries. He'd never been anyone else. He still thought like a Dark Age tyrant. After all this time, he was probably crazier than a cageful of bats, too, but everything he was, everything he defaulted to, was the man who'd been born in a time when a state-of-the-art weapon was a steel sword or a powerful magician. Maybe he really didn't comprehend what a nuclear war would *do* to the world. Maybe he just thought of it as burned crops, leveled cities, and poisoned wells on a mass scale.

"He's still Mordred," Spirit said, realizing. "He's never been anyone else. Not like the others."

"Not like us," Burke said.

Spirit looked at him in surprise. "Us?" she repeated. "Reincarnates?"

"Oh, come on," Loch said. "The odds are at least *one* of us is a former *Knight Who Says Ni*."

"Besides Muirin," Addie said quietly.

"Yeah," Burke said, and after that nobody said anything for a while.

✦

W e're here," Addie said, pulling the van to a halt.

It was a little after noon. Loch had taken over from Burke, and Addie from Loch: Spirit was the only one who didn't know how to drive, and seeing the weariness on her friends' faces that made her feel guilty now. They'd all been awake over twenty-four hours, and to add driving to that. . . .

"Not where I'd choose to make my last stand," Loch said, looking around the parking lot and back at the seedy strip motel.

They'd been seeing signs for Omaha for a while—that and Offutt Air Force Base—but where their directions had led them was to a middle-of-nowhere place that was barely a wide spot in the road: gas station, motel, diner. If there was a town anywhere nearby, or even some random houses, they weren't visible from the Alvo Motor Hotel. There wasn't even a McDonald's.

"Well, there aren't any more directions," Addie said, waving the last sheet of paper. "But. . . . We aren't that far from Omaha. . . ."

"This is where QUERCUS sent us," Spirit said reluctantly. "This is where he'll expect to find us."

"And what then? What do we do then?" Addie asked, a little shrilly. "Is he going to hand us a magic sword? Or turn us into superheroes? Sure, we've got magic—we've *all* got magic—but so do they."

"I know," Spirit said softly. Addie had always doubted their ability—her *own* ability—to fight back, and Spirit really couldn't blame her. "But I don't know what else to do."

"And we're all just about out on our feet," Burke said. "We aren't going anywhere except off the side of the road if we don't get some rest. If this is our only option, well, it's our only option."

"So let's go see what's behind Door Number Six," Loch said.

"Let's go find out if it's locked," Addie said pragmatically.

⭐

Spirit blinked at the brightness of the sunlight as she stepped out of the van. Her shoes—the strappy silver sandals Madison Lane-Rider had picked out as part of her Spring Fling outfit—slid on the asphalt, and she grabbed for the doorframe.

"Easy," Burke said, putting a hand under her arm.

The coat QUERCUS had left for him in the van hung open; the tuxedo beneath it looked jarringly out of place. They were all still wearing their prom clothes under their coats, but at least Spirit's dress was short. Addie was wearing an ankle-length velvet gown; it caught on something as she slid out of the driver's seat, and Spirit heard her snarl as she ripped it free and slammed the door as hard as she could.

"At this point I don't actually care if the Legions of Hell are in there," Loch said, slamming the back door of the van, "as long as I can sit down somewhere that isn't moving."

"Then let's go," Burke said. He released Spirit's arm and walked up to the door. She saw him take a deep breath as he reached for the knob, then he twisted it and the door opened.

The three of them followed him in. The room behind the door matched the outside of the building: worn and shabby. There were two sagging double beds with flowered polyester bedspreads, a nightstand and a lamp, and a dresser. The mirror was cracked in one corner, and there were burns and stains on the dresser top. One of the drawer fronts was slightly askew.

"I'm going to write a stiff letter to the Michelin people," Loch said, walking across the room to sit down on the bed. It creaked and lurched alarmingly when he did so. "Hey," he said, shifting sideways. He picked something up from the bedspread, and held it out so they could all see it. "Looks like we've come to the right place."

Spirit took the oak leaf from his hand. It was fresh and green, like the one they'd found in the van. "Is there anything else here?"

"Not in this," Addie said, quickly opening and closing the dresser drawers. "Unless there's a secret message hidden in the menu of the Alvo Diner," she added, waving a tattered paper menu.

"Nothing here but a Bible," Burke said, closing the drawer of the nightstand. "Not even a phone book."

"Who could there be in this entire state that anybody would want to call?" Loch asked. "So, what now?"

"We wait," Spirit said, pulling off her jacket and sitting down cautiously on the other bed. She'd like to kick her shoes off, but the rug didn't look particularly clean.

"For a while, anyway," Burke said. He tossed his jacket on the bed, followed it with his tuxedo jacket, and sat down beside her. She leaned into him gratefully and he put his arm around her. "And this is as good a place as any to talk about what we do next."

"I didn't know it was open for discussion," Addie grumbled. She sat down on the foot of the bed Loch was on, plucking her skirts up fastidiously.

"Everything's negotiable," Loch said mockingly. "First rule of business. So Mordred's going to start a war, and we've been designated by Spirit's mysterious benefactor as the people who get to stop him. This would seem a lot more stupid if Mordred didn't have magic and can scrub the brain of anybody we tell about his nefarious plans. Of course, he could also just kill them. That'd work."

"Yeah, that's the point," Burke said. "We keep talking about 'stopping' Mordred and his Shadow Knights. I think it's time to admit that 'stop' means 'kill.' Can we do that? This isn't like the Wild Hunt, banishing demons back to Hell or sending Elves back to wherever Elves live. This is killing people, evil or not."

"The good of the many outweighs the good of the few?"

Loch asked lightly. But he couldn't meet Burke's gaze. "I don't know if I could kill someone," he said, staring down at his hands. "Not even knowing. . . ." His voice trailed off.

"I can. I can't just sit here and say I don't want to get my hands dirty knowing what the world will look like if they win."

Spirit's stomach lurched as she spoke. The sound of her own voice frightened her—she didn't sound like anyone she could ever have imagined being. Her heart raced even as she knew she'd meant every word. In her mind was the sound of a gunshot, and Muirin falling. To stop that from happening again? Over and over and over—to millions of people?

She could kill.

"Maybe there's another way," Burke said, hugging her against him. "But I think we should be ready."

"Oh, I'm ready for anything," Addie said bitterly.

❋

They were all too keyed-up to even think of sleeping. There was a little money left from what QUERCUS had left them for gas, so Loch went out to the soda machine and brought back Cokes. After that, there was nothing to do but wait. Everything Spirit could think of to say sounded stupid or useless when she thought about it, and apparently the others felt the same.

What was there to talk about? Muirin was dead, Mordred's Shadow Knights were hunting them, and they were here because they were trusting someone Spirit had met in a secret chat room. And the worst part was, there wasn't anything else they could do.

She was dozing on Burke's shoulder when the sound of the door opening brought her joltingly awake. Loch was already on his feet, and as Spirit rubbed her face with her hands—she and Addie had washed off their makeup as soon as possible—Burke stood as well.

If the woman in the doorway was the rescue party, her looks didn't inspire confidence. She was stray-cat skinny, her frayed jeans and worn parka looked like dumpster treasures, and her brown hair was short and unkempt. Her expression when she looked at them seemed to say she'd expected to see anyone else here but them, but she covered it quickly.

"I'm Vivian," she said. "I'm here to take you to the one you know as Quercus. Let's go."

"Of course," Loch said fulsomely. "Because we're so willing to leave with the first person who shows up with the secret password?"

"That's right," Vivian said evenly. "What choice do you have?"

"Well," Loch said, as if he was considering the matter, "we could stay here. Or you could tell us why we should trust you."

Vivian huffed in exasperation. "Because no matter what you think you know, rich boy, some kids *did* escape from Oakhurst. I did—twenty years ago. Your parents did, too," she added, looking at Burke.

"My parents were murdered by Mordred's *Mafya* hitman," Burke said, taking a step away from Spirit and toward Vivian.

"By Agravaine. Yes," Vivian said, nodding. "But I'm talking about your birth parents, the people who left you in a church, hoping that holy place would protect you, and went willingly to their deaths, knowing they were leading the hunters away from you."

"You knew my parents?" Burke demanded. "My other parents?"

"No," Vivian said. "But Quercus did."

"That's disturbing," Loch said after a moment. "Considering he apparently couldn't protect them."

"You're a chess player," Vivian shot back. "You're aware of the concept of sacrificing a piece to gain the victory."

"Funny," Loch said. "On my planet we call it 'hanging your friends out to dry.' And we've seen a lot of it from the Shadow Knights lately."

"Good for you," Vivian said, sounding even more irritated. "But I don't intend to stand around here all day dispelling your ignorance. I'm here to take you to Quercus. Now get moving. Or don't, and wait for them to catch up with you. Your choice."

Addie glanced from Loch to Vivian, her mouth set in a thin line of resentment. Spirit looked up at Burke. He was frowning, but he looked more confused than angry.

"Come on," Spirit said with a resigned sigh. "We don't have a lot of choices. If she was a Shadow Knight, she'd already have tried to kill us. Or something."

"If—" Addie began. "I—"

"Move it," Vivian said. "If you want to hang around outside here like idiot bait, I don't." She turned around and walked out, leaving the door open.

"Nice lady," Loch said, but he was already reaching for his coat.

When they got to the van, Vivian was already in the driver's seat. "Back's open," she said.

They looked at each other. "I'll ride up front," Loch said. "That way we can find our way back here if we have to." Loch's primary Gift was Shadewalking—the ability to move silently and undetected—but he had a secondary Gift of Pathfinding: the ability to always know exactly where he was, and to find his way unerringly from place to place. He climbed into the van on the passenger side, and the rest of them went around to the back. Burke helped Spirit and Addie up into the van and closed the door.

"This is our only vehicle," Vivian said, over the sound of the engine. "I've been in the area since last night. I wanted to make sure they weren't using Scrying Mages to set up an ambush. We're good, though. I'm guessing they don't want any of their people getting a peek at the endgame." She backed and turned the van, and then they were heading down the road again.

"If the van is your only way of getting around," Addie said, "and you left it for us, how did you get back here?"

"Hitchhiked," Vivian said. "If you were expecting G.I. Joe and his secret underwater base, think again."

"'Knowing is half the battle,'" Burke muttered, quoting. He sounded worried.

They drove for another hour. Vivian ignored all of their attempts to find out anything about her, about QUERCUS, or about what was going to happen next. They stayed on the back roads, and the countryside looked even more deserted, if possible, than what they'd driven through to get here. If Omaha was somewhere around here, it was doing a good job of hiding.

At last Vivian turned down a narrow side road, and they could see they were approaching something that looked military.

And abandoned. There were faded and splintered No Trespassing signs everywhere. The only fence was a tangle of rusted barbed wire, and nothing was paved. Vivian drove through a gap in the coils and up to a cluster of tarpaper shacks that looked like they'd been deserted since before Spirit had been born: doors open or missing entirely, holes in the roof, siding stripped away to expose the framing beneath.

Spirit's heart sank. *What if this is all some kind of . . . delusion? What if QUERCUS doesn't exist? All I have to go on is the Ironkey, and Vivian could've made that. She could have been QUERCUS, too. There's no way to know. And if she's crazy, if this whole idea of taking out the Shadow Knights is just some kind of . . . fantasy. . . .*

Vivian pulled up behind one of the shacks. "End of the line," she said. When everyone was out of the van, she picked up a camo net hanging from the back of the shack and dragged the loose side over the van.

"Where are we?" Burke asked, looking around.

"Nebraska," Vivian said. "I don't suppose any of you know history, but a long time ago—before any of us was born—the US was expecting to go to war with Russia."

"I *have* heard of the Cold War," Loch said dryly.

"Then you know they figured on fighting it with missiles," Vivian said. "Intercontinental Ballistic Missiles—ICBMs. They launched from silos. There were hundreds of them—thousands—all over the country. The areas they were located in were called 'missile fields.' About thirty years ago, they started decommissioning the missiles. They were obsolete. But there isn't much you can do with a former missile silo."

"Except call it home," Burke said.

"Got it in one. Come on."

She led them into the shack she'd parked behind. It was completely trashed—broken windows, holes in the roof, leaves, glass, and unidentifiable trash on the floor. There was an old steel desk in one corner, turned on its side. The linoleum floor had been ripped up in places, and underneath was a concrete slab. Addie held her skirt up carefully, and Spirit wished she was wearing something sturdier on her feet than sandals.

Vivian led them into the second room. It was dark—there were black plastic garbage bags taped over the windows—and in the middle was a large hole in the floor. It looked to Spirit like one of those big storm drains—the opening was more than three feet across, and there were steel rungs set into one side.

"Who wants to go first?" Vivian said.

"None of us," Addie said fervently.

"I'll go first," Loch said. "You next," he said to Addie. "Be careful in those shoes."

Addie made a face.

Loch walked over and just jumped in. Spirit yelped in dismay until she saw he'd grabbed one of the rungs before he could fall. "There's lights at the bottom," he called up, then they heard the scraping of his shoes on the rungs as he climbed quickly down.

"Showoff," Burke muttered. "I'll lift you in," he said to Addie.

Her face was grim, but she nodded. He picked her up as if she weighed nothing, and lowered her carefully until she could grab the rungs. She looked up at him, nodded, and began to descend.

"Maybe you should go next," Burke said to Vivian.

"Maybe I should stay up here to make sure you two don't bolt," Vivian said. Burke just shook his head and turned to Spirit. "Ready?" he asked.

She forced herself to nod. He picked her up and held her over the opening in the floor the way he had Addie. The sense of emptiness under her feet, the knowledge that Burke's grip on her arms—and hers on his—was the only thing that kept her from falling—maybe to her death—was terrifying. She forced herself to let go and reach for one of the rungs in front of her. It was cold and a little slick under her hands. She kicked until she had her feet placed securely, took a deep breath, and Burke let go.

It's just a ladder, Spirit told herself. *You've climbed a lot of ladders.*

But not blind, and not in the dark. She forced herself to feel for the next rung, and began her careful descent. When she'd gone down a few feet, the light from above was blocked as Burke followed her into the shaft, and a few seconds later she heard Loch call up that he'd reached the bottom.

It seemed like a long way down. When she got there, she saw the bottom of the shaft was lit by wire-covered lights on the walls. In the wall there was a metal door standing open. It looked like it belonged on a submarine. Loch and Addie were standing just inside.

"I know what this is," Loch said, as she walked in. The room was fairly large—maybe twenty feet long—and the ceiling was so far up Spirit couldn't see it clearly. "It's a launch bunker. It's where the missile crews would wait for orders to launch—see? There's the computers and the monitors," he said, pointing at a bank of equipment on one wall. It looked like something out of an ancient Science Fiction movie.

"Their regular tours were only twelve hours, but in the event of actual war they would've had to stay down here for days. So there's a whole apartment down here." Loch gestured toward a battered couch on the wall opposite the computers. On that wall there were two doorways that clearly led to other rooms.

There was no one else here.

"How is it you know these things?" Addie asked.

"I'm a guy," Loch said, shrugging. "I thought it was kind of cool. You know, in an Armageddon, nuclear holocaust, *Planet of the Apes* way."

There was a thump from outside, and Burke walked in. "Whoa," he said, looking around.

"Best secret clubhouse ever," Loch said, deadpan.

"I thought we were supposed to stop a war, not start one," Burke answered.

"You are," Vivian said. She pulled the metal door closed behind her. From the way she moved, it was heavy, but it moved silently. There was a wheel in the middle of it on the inside, just like in every submarine movie Spirit had ever seen.

"Where's QUERCUS?" Spirit demanded. "We're the only ones here, aren't we?"

"I need to tell you a story," Vivian said, not answering her directly. She pulled off her jacket and walked over to the couch.

"If this is some kind of trick. . . ." Burke rumbled threateningly.

"Why would I bother?" Vivian demanded angrily. "If I'd wanted you dead, all I'd have to do would be make one phone call while you were waiting for me to show up. I get that you don't trust me—I spent two years at Oakhurst before I figured out what was going on. I know what it's like."

Spirit moved over to Burke and took his hand. She didn't know what to think. She didn't believe this was a trap, not really, but when she'd decided to trust QUERCUS's escape plan, she'd been counting on there being something more substantial at the end of it than an abandoned missile silo. Set against the resources of Oakhurst, of Breakthrough, this was . . . nothing.

"How did you find out?" Addie asked unexpectedly. "About Mordred, and . . . everything?"

"I'm a Water Witch like you," Vivian answered. "One day several of us were practicing down at the pool. One of my teammates hit me with a waterspout. It knocked me off my feet. I fell into the pool, hitting my head on the way in. I pretty much drowned before someone pulled me out. And after that, I . . . remembered."

"You're a Reincarnate," Spirit said.

"If I hadn't been, I'd be dead," Vivian said. "I'd known Mordred . . . before . . . but I didn't recognize him at first. None of us do, I think, even after we remember. He isn't a Reincarnate—Merlin's spell made sure of that. But he possessed some biker named Kenny Hawking. That's the body he's wearing now."

"That part we'd pieced together ourselves," Addie said. "But—"

"Merlin? Spell?" Loch interrupted.

"Look, if I don't tell this in order you'll be even more confused than you are now. Long story short: I knew who *I* was, I figured out who *he* was, I ran like hell and went looking for Merlin. It helped that Mordred hadn't gathered as many of his Shadow Knights as he has now. I wouldn't have been able to escape if I'd had to do it today."

Spirit shuddered. They'd only gotten away from Oakhurst

with a lot of help, and being away from Oakhurst didn't mean safe.

"And you found Merlin," Spirit said. "QUERCUS. QUERCUS is Merlin, isn't he?"

Vivian nodded. "Yes. But let me start at the beginning. It's a long story. Make yourselves comfortable."

Addie sat down on the couch beside Vivian. There were two chairs in front of the computer console. Loch took one, and Spirit took the other. Burke remained standing, his arms folded across his chest.

"You probably know something about King Arthur and Camelot and all that, but what you know isn't the way it really was. There were two great Queens who ruled over the land: the *Bán Steud* and the *Cú Dubh*."

"The White Mare and the Black Hound," Addie said. Certainly Oakhurst had crammed their heads with enough languages that a little Gaelic wasn't much of a stretch.

"Yes. In those days the Power ran hot and free in the pillars of the earth, and it was the birthright of many, and so Guinevere, the White Mare's Daughter, and Morgause, the Black Hound, were both women of power. Britain was Guinevere's by ancient right, and Morgause meant to take it from her."

"Sounds like *Mists of Avalon* to me," Loch said. "Where does Arthur come into it?"

"He was the brother of Morgause and the uncle of Mordred," Vivian answered. "Morgause had always meant to rule Britain through either her brother or her son, but she lost Arthur to Belcadrus—to the army, you would say—and after a time he became *Diuc Bán Tir*, Duke of Britain. When Arthur passed beyond her influence, Morgause concentrated all her arts upon her son. Mordred became a black necromancer, steeped in the darkest sorceries, but his uncle knew nothing of this, because Mordred concealed his true nature, believing he would be named Arthur's heir—as much as Arthur could have an heir, since he wasn't king."

"But, uh, Duke of Britain?" Loch said, glancing apologetically at Spirit and shrugging. "That's the same thing, right?"

Vivian shook her head. "Britain had more kings than—than Justin Bieber has fangirls. But it had no true king—High King—because for generations none of the White Mare's daughters had chosen to wed."

"I thought Arthur married Guinevere," Burke said, frowning as if he suspected Vivian of trying to trick him.

"He did," Vivian said impatiently. "Guinevere was the White Mare's Daughter, and only marriage to her could confer the High Kingship. Arthur waited years, refusing to marry, and at last his patience was rewarded, for in the darkest hour of his battle against the Saxons, Guinevere came to him on the battlefield, bringing with her the white horses of Britain. The tide was turned, Arthur won the victory, and The Merlin came to Camelot to make the wedding. Mordred knew he could not conceal his true nature from The Merlin, nor could he hope—now—to be named Arthur's royal heir. He spoke fair words—as they said in those days—and went far from the court."

"I know how this story goes," Loch said impatiently.

"No, you don't. That's the trouble," Vivian answered immediately. "Arthur wasn't king because he won a lot of fights. He was king because he was Guinevere's husband, and *whoever* her husband was would be High King. Mordred meant to marry her, and that meant she must break her marriage to Arthur and choose another husband. Choose *him*."

Spirit listened impatiently. All of this was ancient history—literally. No matter what the details were, they knew how it ended: with Mordred locked up in an oak tree, and the Round Table doomed to be reborn over and over until Mordred was dead. She opened her mouth to protest. Vivian smirked, as if she'd heard Spirit's every thought. Spirit flushed, and forced herself to stay silent. *But if she doesn't start telling us something useful soon, I'm going to—*

"Years passed," Vivian went on, as if she didn't notice Spirit's impatience. "Acting in secret, Mordred stripped Arthur of his true knights and advisors. Lancelot was tricked into leaving Camelot. The Merlin was imprisoned in an enchanted oak. By then Arthur knew the shape of his doom, but he could see no way to prevent it—he might hold Britain, but both he and the White Mare's Daughter could die as easily as any other. But Guinevere told him he could prevail by seeming to fall to Mordred's treachery, and together they formed a plan. Before all the Court, he named her faithless and banished her—so all believed—to Glastonbury Abbey. But she went to Avalon instead, and there she gathered an army that could fight Mordred with sorcery."

Spirit fidgeted. None of this seemed particularly important

now. And no matter how much Vivian said it was the unknown story of Camelot, it all seemed very familiar. Had she dreamed this? Or read it? Either way, she *did* know how Vivian's tale ended. *Arthur dead, Mordred fled, and Guinevere chases him until she catches him. Tell me something I don't know.* With a real effort, she kept herself from tapping her foot and tried to pay attention.

Finally her frustration became too much. "And Merlin imprisoned him in Gallows Oak because Mordred couldn't be killed," she blurted. "But Mordred did something to Merlin. And Guinevere said she and her army would keep watch over Mordred and his allies forever. And that's where the Reincarnates—the Shadow Knights and the Grail Knights—come from. How does this help us *now?*"

Burke looked toward her in surprise, but Vivian seemed to have expected Spirit's outburst. "The spell Mordred cast bound The Merlin's spirit to his flesh until the end of time. He would never be reborn," Vivian said.

"But that was centuries ago—and Merlin isn't dead," Spirit protested, when Vivian didn't say anything else.

"Yes," Vivian said. "Mordred's spell struck true, but The Merlin was more powerful than he had dreamed. If The Merlin would not be reborn, neither would he die. Centuries passed. The Merlin became a wraith, a spirit. The ancient Gifts we once took for granted passed out of common keeping, and he could not make himself known to anyone. Until a few decades ago." She smiled as if she was about to tell them an unfunny joke. "First ARPANET, then NIPRNET, then NSFNET . . . electrical pulses, binary code, something he could influence to give himself a voice again."

"You are not saying that Merlin has taken over the Internet," Addie said flatly. "You really aren't."

Even Loch was speechless.

"Not 'taken over,'" Vivian said. "He speaks through it."

"Oh, that—that's *completely different*," Loch said, sounding as if he didn't know whether to laugh or start yelling. "That's completely reasonable. Of course there's a dead Druid in the Internet. It explains everything."

"The ghost in the machine," Addie said. She gave a blurt of laughter and looked horrified.

They looked at each other. Loch looked incredulous, Addie looked shocked, Burke actually looked irritated. Spirit had no idea what expression was on her own face, but she felt . . . boggled. Even finding out magic was real hadn't been this much of a shock. Merlin was a computer program. It was a cliché and unbelievable at the same time.

"Well," Burke said after a very long pause. "I guess it isn't any weirder than being in the middle of a battle between Merlin and Mordred surrounded by a bunch of reincarnated Arthurian knights."

Loch stared at him in pained disbelief. Burke shrugged.

"So Mordred takes over a biker and Merlin takes over the Internet and our side is losing?" Loch asked.

"Not 'taken over,'" Vivian repeated irritably. "He—"

"Is. . . . Can I talk to him?" Spirit finally asked.

"I was waiting for somebody to grow a brain," Vivian muttered. She went over to the bank of computers and began flipping switches. Lights came on, and the room was filled with a low whooshing hum.

It sounds like it's going to blow up. Or break, Spirit thought.

"Planning to start World War Last?" Loch asked.

"There aren't any missiles here and I don't have the launch codes anyway. But I do have Internet."

It took a while for the equipment to warm up, but when it did, letters appeared on both of the CRT screens.

HELLO SPIRIT. I AM GLAD YOU AND YOUR FRIENDS ARRIVED SAFELY. WE HAVE MUCH WORK TO DO.

Spirit had stood up when Vivian came over. Now Vivian gestured brusquely toward the seat she'd vacated. "He can see us, but he can't hear us. You'll have to type to talk to him."

Spirit sat down and turned to face the monitor. A green cursor blinked like a heartbeat. She poised her fingers over the keys, hesitating. Despite everything—despite Oakhurst's lessons in paranoia—she believed this was QUERCUS. She'd trusted him before, and she'd trust him now. But what could she say?

The keyboard was large and awkward—it took pressure to strike the keys, and they clicked loudly as she did. HELLO, QUERCUS, she typed.

Suddenly it was all too much for her. She burst into tears, choking back sobs and shaking her head to clear away the tears she wouldn't stop to wipe away.

MUIRIN IS DEAD AND SHE DIED TO PROTECT US, AND DOC MAC IS DEAD AND WE KNOW WHAT

MORDRED'S PLANNING NOW AND WE HAVE TO STOP
HIM AND I DON'T KNOW HOW

Words appeared on the screen beneath hers.

I HAVE PREPARED FOR THIS BATTLE FOR MANY
YEARS. NOW YOU AND YOUR FRIENDS MUST FIGHT
ONCE AGAIN. WEAPONS HAVE BEEN PREPARED FOR
YOU, AND FOR THIS DAY. YOU MUST SEEK THEM OUT.
VIVIAN WILL HELP YOU.

She scrubbed at her eyes, trying to stop crying. He was
asking the impossible. They were all there was? Four teenagers against the hosts of Hell?

Burke put an arm across her shoulders, and silently offered
a handkerchief. She wiped her face and blew her nose. "It
doesn't matter," she whispered. *It doesn't matter if we can't win.
We'll be dead when Mordred starts his war whether we fight back
now or not. So we might as well die trying to stop him.*

She swallowed hard and typed: TELL US WHAT WE
NEED TO DO.

There was a pause, as if the mind on the other side of the
screen was considering.

REST NOW.

The words—his and hers—disappeared from the screen,
leaving only the blinking green cursor.

The others had gathered around Spirit as she typed, watching the screen. She looked up. Addie's eyes were wet with tears
and Loch looked miserable.

"I never backed off from a fight just because I didn't think I could win," Burke said slowly, but Spirit could tell he was troubled.

"I don't think we have much choice," Loch said. He sounded strained—angry. *He's come to the same conclusion I have,* Spirit thought. *Refusing to fight won't save us.*

"Why this?" Addie demanded. "Why us? There are only four of us—Breakthrough has hundreds of people! How can he possibly think we can win?"

"Because you're *special*," Vivian said mockingly, and none of them could tell whether she meant it as a joke. "And the 'weapons' Merlin's talking about are pretty powerful. That's why he had to hide them. If he hadn't, Mordred would've found them a long time ago. Not even he knows where they are now."

"Oh, great. To avert the end of the world we have to go on a *treasure hunt* first?" Loch snapped.

It hurt to smile, but Spirit did anyway. She could always count on Loch to be indignant about things that were just plain terrifying—and come right out with what everyone was thinking and didn't want to say.

"Welcome to my world," Vivian said dryly. "But right now, you need to get some sleep—and out of those stupid clothes. I'll show you to your spacious accommodations."

two

Vivian pointed things out as she led them down the hall—kitchen, toilets, showers, something she called a "ready room." The bedroom was a little smaller than the outer room, and contained two sets of bunk beds. There was a big schoolroom-type clock on the wall, and the speakers for the old PA system—rusty now—were tucked up in the corners of the ceiling. The room had no door, just a curtain you could pull across the doorway. There were footlockers at the foot of each bed.

"Clothes," Vivian said, pointing. "You should be able to find something that fits. Even you, big guy. Sleep well."

She walked out. Spirit felt overwhelmed, numb. Too tired to feel anything, really. Except maybe a little relief, because at least they were presumably safe enough to sleep. After a moment, Addie walked over and pulled the curtain shut.

"Well, this sucks," Loch said comprehensively, sticking his hands in his pockets. His formal clothes, rumpled as they were, looked completely out of place here. "I thought we were joining the Rebel Alliance. Turns out we *are* the Rebel Alliance."

"Yeah, well, no matter how bad it is, it's got to be better than being at Oakhurst right now," Burke said. He opened the nearer of the two footlockers. Spirit didn't know what she'd expected to see—uniforms?—but instead it was filled with regular clothes. There were several small plastic bags on top. He tossed one to Loch and began pulling out clothes, holding them up to check the sizes.

"All the comforts of home," Loch said, opening the bag and brandishing a toothbrush. "If your home happens to be a minimum security prison, of course."

"You'll notice I didn't get an answer to my question," Addie said, going over to the other chest and rummaging through it. "We aren't— We aren't *superheroes.* And I don't think I trust that— That *Vivian.*"

Spirit sat down on one of the bunks. At least it had sheets and blankets, and she wasn't going to have to worry about creepy crawlies in them. You couldn't say as much for that motel. "We're pretty much out of choices," she said wearily, her shoulders sagging. "How would we feel knowing we could do something to— To *fix* things— And we didn't?"

"Well, gosh," Loch said poisonously, "I guess we'd all feel pretty bad about that, Spirit. But at least it wouldn't be for long. Six weeks from now Mordred starts World War Three. And I'm betting wherever this is, it's a first strike zone."

"Yeah," Burke said meditatively, ignoring the sarcasm. He tossed a sweatshirt and a pair of pants up to the top bunk, unrolled a pair of white sweat socks to check the size, and added them to the pile. "A lot of the silos in the old 'missile fields' are decommissioned, but not all of them. And there's a couple of military bases in this area. First strike zone."

"But. . . . I thought Mordred was going to launch the missiles *here*," Addie said. She handed Loch a bundle of clothing and held up a worn pink sweater, grimacing. "You know—at us, this country. So why would it matter if our own missiles were being fired and landing here?"

"Doesn't matter, because this stuff is set up so that when there's a bird in the air, everyone goes berserk," Burke said simply. "Once any of them hits—anywhere—everybody's going to be pointing fingers. And the fingers are going to be pushing buttons."

"Maybe somebody should mention that to Mordred," Loch said. Burke just snorted.

But Spirit's thoughts had moved sluggishly on. "QUER—*Merlin* said 'again,'" Spirit said. "He said we must fight *once again*." She looked up at Burke, at Addie and Loch.

"And now for that new hit reality show, *Guess Which Arthurian Character You Used To Be*," Loch said in fulsome tones. "Because if you still think we aren't all Reincarnates, you clearly don't get out much."

"I don't *want* to be somebody else!" Addie wailed. She slammed the lid of the chest and sat down on it.

"Maybe we aren't," Spirit said, though she didn't really

42

believe it herself. "Maybe it's like me not having magic at Oakhurst—maybe we've been picked because we *aren't* Reincarnates."

"I wish," Loch said, sighing. "My idea of fun isn't riding around looking for something to hit with a big sword. And I'm not sure those guys ever did anything else. And, gee, swords versus SMGs? Guess who wins."

"Actually," Burke said, "we've got a bigger problem than that."

"Oh, bring it," Addie said, waving her hand.

"Sweatpants," Burke said, holding several pairs up.

"Sweatpants are our problem?" Loch asked.

"No. Sweatpants to sleep in," Burke said, tossing one set at Loch. "It's cold down here. Our problem is this: can Merlin still do magic now that he's in the computer? And if he can't—and if we're Reincarnates—how do we get our memories back? Without our memories, I'm not sure we can do anything at all."

"Burke!" Spirit said, in automatic protest. She ran her hands through her hair, her head spinning with too many questions and no answers at all. It was actually making her feel sick, and her head was starting to pound. "I just— I'm so tired. . . ." She didn't want to think about any of this right now. She thought Loch was right, and they were all Reincarnates, and the thought of having somebody else's life stuffed into her mind . . . how would that not be like dying? And how would it *help?*

"I'm sorry," Burke said contritely. "I shouldn't've said anything."

"Oh, Vivian will probably have an answer," Addie said, acidly. She got up and opened the chest again. "But right now I'm getting out of this stupid dress. And I wish I was a Fire Witch, because I'd like to burn it."

She turned and walked out, her arms full of clothes.

"These look about your size," Burke said, handing Spirit a sweatshirt and a pair of sweatpants. "I guess right now we do what Vivian says. If she's been hiding from Mordred as long as she says she has, she can't be stupid."

"No," Spirit said, wrapping her arms around the bundle of cloth. The items were old and worn, bringing back memories of Goodwill expeditions with her family, but they smelled clean. "I don't think she's stupid. I'm just wondering if she's crazy."

✦

They'd gone one by one to the bathroom to change and to brush their teeth. Spirit thought it was a little weird sleeping in the same room with Burke and Loch, even though the sweatshirts and sweatpants covered all of them more thoroughly than the gym clothes she'd seen both boys in a thousand times. When Loch shut off the lights, the darkness seemed absolute until her eyes adjusted, then she could see a faint glow of light through the door curtain. Burke and Loch took the top bunks, she and Addie had the bottom ones.

Spirit was so tired she ached, and her head was still throbbing, but she didn't think she could possibly sleep.

"Goodnight, John Boy," Loch said suddenly.

"I can't believe you ever watched that show," Addie said.

"Hey, when you've spent as many days in random hotel rooms as I have, you become a connoisseur of stupid Seventies television," Loch answered.

"Yeah, whatever," Burke said. "Shut up and go to sleep."

And in the silence that followed, somehow Spirit did.

⁂

The wind was cold, whipping her hair and pulling her cloak away from her shoulders. She could smell the coming winter on the air.

I'm dreaming, Spirit thought. She struggled to open her eyes—not to wake up, but to take control of her dream. Lucid dreaming was one of the many things they taught at Oakhurst. It interlocked with many of the Schools and Gifts, but you could do it even if you didn't have magic.

Why didn't I ever try this before? she thought. *I've had this dream before, I know I have.*

In the way of dreams, she *knew* what was around her—open land, grass and morning sunlight—but she couldn't *see* it. She struggled to open her eyes and see what was around her, but the only thing that changed was what she could hear. Over the rustling of the wind, she heard a woman's voice shouting for her to hurry, to awake, the battle was joined and it was almost too late. . . .

With a last effort, Spirit forced her dream-self to open its eyes. She caught a glimpse of a horse—impossibly large and impossibly white—with a rider, a woman, her face contorted with urgency. She was the one whose cries Spirit had heard, and Spirit opened her mouth to answer, but when she moved, the dream twisted and jumbled and vanished. Instead of cold wind in her hair, she felt the lumpy hardness of the mattress at her back, and the air was still and metal-smelling.

She was awake.

She tried to hold onto the fragments of the dream—to make sense of them—but they were already becoming vague and meaningless. A woman on a horse, telling her to hurry. *I've dreamed about her a lot since the February Dance,* Spirit thought, frowning. *Is she a Reincarnate? Is she me? Who is she? I wish they all came with labels. . . .*

The idea that she was a Reincarnate was somehow even more disturbing than knowing she'd gotten her magic—not that she had any idea of what it *was.* Maybe Vivian or Merlin could help. . . .

The last of the dream faded. She realized the lights were on, and she could smell breakfast—somebody was frying bacon and toasting bread. The smell reminded Spirit that she hadn't eaten in an awfully long time. She opened her eyes, swung her feet over the side of the bunk, and sat up cautiously.

Addie was still in bed asleep, her black hair spilling across her face as she clutched her pillow. The bunk above—where Loch had slept—was empty. When Spirit got to her feet, she saw Burke's bunk was empty, too. They were probably where the food was. She sorted quickly through the clothes they'd left in such a mess last night, and found a pair of jeans that looked like they'd fit, and the disco-is-dead pink sweater Addie had rejected last night: it had a wide V neck, and a bunch of glittery silver bits woven into it, but at least it wasn't in the Oakhurst colors, and it was warm. There were even a pair of canvas slip-ons she could wear—years of shopping in second-hand stores had made her a good judge of sizes. And Burke had found socks last night for both of them. She bundled the garments up with a sigh before sorting through the underwear. None of it was really in her size, and there weren't any bras at all. She was stuck with the one from her prom outfit, and it was strapless.

As she went down the hall to the bathroom, she could hear voices coming from the kitchen. She washed and dressed, and when she went back to the bedroom to make the bed and dump the other clothes, Addie was starting to stir.

"Breakfast," Spirit said. Addie groaned and rolled over. Spirit glanced at the clock. It said it was six, but whether it was six in the morning or six at night, she didn't know. "Come on," she said, with a cheer she didn't feel. "You don't want to miss the Apocalypse."

Addie groaned again, and felt around on the floor for something to throw. She didn't find anything, and rolled over on her back. "This is your brain. This is your brain on magic. Any questions?" she muttered.

"Bacon," Spirit said.

"I hate you," Addie answered, but she started moving. Spirit went off in search of the kitchen.

✦

"—computer programmer. It's the kind of thing I can do remotely, and I only have to go into the city once or twice a month to pick up my mail and cash my checks," Vivian said.

The kitchen was tiny, with a two-burner electric stove and a table crammed into one corner. Loch was perched on the table, and Burke was crammed into one corner, watching Vivian cook. They were both wearing hand-me-downs—Burke in sweatpants and a T-shirt, Loch in jeans. Loch was wearing the shirt from his prom outfit, with the collar unbuttoned and the sleeves rolled up. There was already a pile of crispy bacon draining on a plate, and Spirit's stomach rumbled. The sandwiches in the van seemed like at least a week ago.

"Hi," she said a little uncertainly.

"Morning," Vivian said. "Breakfast will be ready in a couple of minutes, so you better go wake up Addie."

"She was moving when I left," Spirit said.

Burke smiled at her and handed her a piece of toast; Spirit nibbled it to give herself something to do. A moment later Addie joined them. She was wearing jeans and a red sweater with a pattern of green Christmas trees knitted into it. Spirit winced sympathetically.

"Cozy," Addie said, looking around.

"These places were designed for two sets of two-man crews,"

Vivian said, "so it's going to be a little crowded in the kitchen with five."

"So what's on the menu for today?" Loch asked. "Besides breakfast."

"I tell you the rest of what Merlin needs you to know, and then I'm headed into town. I didn't want to lay in a bunch of stuff until I was sure you'd get here alive."

Spirit repressed a shudder of unease at Vivian's matter-of-factness. "What. . . . What would you have done if we hadn't?"

"Yeah, considering we're apparently all there is in the way of opposition to Mordred's evil plot," Loch said.

"Get used to it," Vivian said. She put the last of the bacon on the plate and tucked it into the tiny oven. "If the plan to get you out of there had failed, I would've done whatever I could to bring the Feds down on Breakthrough. There probably wouldn't've been much of Montana left when the dust settled, but it would be better than the end of the world. Assuming, of course, that they listened to me, and the Feds won."

"It still sounds like a better option than us against Breakthrough," Burke said. "So why not do it anyway? As a backup?"

"Because it would lead Breakthrough straight here," Vivian said. "Mordred's stuck in the Dark Ages, but his Shadow Knights aren't. If Mark doesn't have a snitch in one of the Alphabet Agencies, I'd be really surprised."

"But—" Loch said.

"And there's even odds Breakthrough could put out enough black information on me to make the Feds ignore anything I had to say," Vivian said, taking out the carton of eggs and beginning to crack them into the skillet. "And Mordred knows about it." She sighed irritably. "Just before Eternal September, when everybody found out about the Internet. . . ." She paused, clearly choosing her words carefully. "My dad was a phone phreak. I grew up learning how to program—and hack— computers. So one day a bunch of Men in Black show up at the house and we all get dragged off to jail. That was the last time I ever saw my parents. Nobody would tell me anything about what was happening and meanwhile, I'm sitting in Juvie—fourteen, no relatives, you do the math. So this slick Oakhurst creep shows up and says my mom sent him and I get to come live at Oakhurst until the whole legal thing is set-tled. My mom knew some weird people, so it seemed almost reasonable—and anyway, I thought any place would be better than Juvenile Hall, right? So I get to Oakhurst, find out— surprise!—I'm a Teen Witch, and about a month later I get called into Mordred's office and he tells me my parents want me to stay at Oakhurst where I'll be safe." She broke off, staring silently into space for a moment before picking up the spatula and starting to flip the eggs.

"Oakhurst had a computer center even back then, and once I'd settled in, I started phreaking the line to dial out to my old BBSs. When I talked to people, they didn't believe I was me—everyone'd heard my mom, my dad, and me were all dead. And I knew it was true, because my parents would have posted if they were alive, and they didn't." She shrugged. "I figured 'Doctor Ambrosius' just didn't tell me the truth because he was afraid I'd flip out. I spent a lot of time online—there wasn't any kind of firewall or anything back then; this was the early nineties, remember—and that's where I met Merlin. I thought he was just another hacker, but he was nice. After I got my other memories back, I was pretty desperate—the 'problem' kids were going missing and I was pretty sure I was on the list. He told me how to get out of Oakhurst without being grabbed by the Wild Hunt, and where to find him. And here we are. Breakfast's ready."

⁂

So you've been living underground all this time?" Addie asked, when they were settled in the monitor room with their food.

"Merlin helped me papertrip myself," Vivian said. "Including the academic credentials I needed to get work—at least, once I looked old enough to have been to college. But once I try to blow the whistle on Oakhurst, the first thing the Shadow Knights are going to do is drag up the ancient history and convince the Feds I'm a cyber-terrorist."

"If they can find you," Burke said.

"They would," Vivian said darkly. "And that means they'd find you, too. So we'll try this Merlin's way first."

"Which is what, exactly?" Loch asked. "Finding these 'secret weapons' Merlin's hidden so carefully even *he* can't find them?"

"If he knew where they were—or for that matter, if they

stayed in the same place for very long—anybody with Scrying Gift could locate them eventually. Since they can't, we're hoping Mordred thinks they're lost."

"But what are they? And how do they work?" Spirit could hardly believe she was asking these questions, but what other choices did they have? *And what makes you and Merlin so sure the four of us can use them?*

"They're the Four Hallows of Britain: the Sword, the Shield, the Cauldron—or Cup—and the Lance. Spear, you'd say. The Cup heals anything placed in it, and can provide whatever you most need—"

"Must be a pretty big cup," Loch muttered. Vivian shot him a poisonous look.

"—the Sword confers victory on the wielder, the Lance can pierce any object it's cast at—and the Shield cannot be breached by spell or by weapon. Merlin managed to get them to America, but without their proper guardians, they radiate enough magic to be instantly perceptible to Mordred. So Merlin hid them. Or, more precisely, told them to hide themselves. Find them, and you're all set."

"You aren't telling us everything," Spirit said after a moment.

Vivian looked at her with an expression of grudging respect. "I'm telling you everything you need to know," she said. "You'll understand the rest when you have the Hallows."

"So where do we start looking?" Spirit asked.

"Yeah, seeing as we're kind of on-the-clock here," Loch said. "First of May, Armageddon Day!"

"Too bad," Vivian said. "I told you: I don't know where

they are, and neither does Merlin. They have to find you. There's this thing about them: they find their rightful owners. Which should be you. If you aren't and they don't, well, then we're screwed and I've already told you how well Plan B is likely to work."

There was a moment of disbelieving silence, and then Addie, Loch, and even Burke all started talking at once. Yelling, really. This was ridiculous, this was unfair, the four of them against all of Mordred's Shadow Knights—and people with guns—and all they were getting were a sword and a spear and they weren't even getting those, they had to go looking for them and nobody knew where—

"What if they're in California?" Loch demanded. "Or Vermont? What if they've gone back to England? *What if Breakthrough grabs us while we're looking for them?*"

"How are we even supposed to try to do something if all you're going to do is put more obstacles in our way?" Addie shouted, near tears. "It's like you *want* us to lose!"

"What if we don't find them in time?" Burke bellowed. "How do we even use them once we find them? I "

"*We don't have any choice!*" Spirit screamed at the top of her lungs.

Suddenly the room was dead silent.

"We don't have any choice," she repeated more quietly. "You've all spent your time *doing* magic. Well, all I've been able to do until yesterday was *study* it—and I still have no idea what these so-called 'School of Spirit' powers are, or what they're going to actually do for me. But what I *do* know is that you can't argue with magic. You just can't. You have to do things its way, and I happen to think that sucks. But you can't *argue* with it. It won't listen. So. . . . I guess I won't blame any of you if you don't want to do this. But I'm going to go look for these Hallows. And hope."

None of the others would look at her except Vivian, and Spirit couldn't tell what Vivian was thinking. *All Merlin said was that when their wielders were found, they'd appear.* It wasn't particularly helpful, but Vivian insisted she didn't know anything more. Spirit had the strangest feeling that now that they'd gotten here, Vivian was content to let the four of them make all the decisions—which would have worked out a lot better if any of them had the slightest idea of what to do. *We're just kids, for crying out loud! In the real world, no one would expect us to make a decision about what car to buy, much less something like this! And what if we aren't the "wielders" the Four Hallows are looking for? What then?*

She wondered if they'd taught the Fifth School of Magic when Vivian had been at Oakhurst. Doc Mac had known about it. He'd said it "dealt primarily with gifts of mental control and influence" which made it sound pretty creepy. And dangerous. She took a deep breath. *You don't have time to think about that now. Even if thinking about it is a lot better than thinking about the four of us being the only ones on Merlin's side. . . .*

Loch finally broke the silence. "Muirin would have liked to be here," he said softly. "And she can't be. So I don't want to do this—like, a *lot*—but I'm going to."

"Me too," Burke said unhesitatingly.

"I think it's useless and it won't work, even if we find these 'Hallows,'" Addie said in exasperation. "But. . . . I'm in. Muirin was the first real friend I ever had. And they killed her."

In that moment, Spirit loved all of them more than she ever had before. This was ridiculous—like playing a game of Candyland against Death for the fate of the world—but no matter what her friends thought, they were all willing to try.

"So," Spirit said, turning to Vivian. "How do we . . . let them find us?"

※

We've got about an hour before we meet up with Vivian," Burke said, stopping the van in the parking lot. Spirit resisted the urge to look around for danger as she got out. She knew she wouldn't see the Shadow Knights coming: Shade-walkers and Illusionists could both make themselves pretty much invisible. If Breakthrough found them, they were toast.

"Vivian said to meet her at the Bess Streeter Aldrich House and Museum," Loch said, waving the map Vivian had given them. "Anybody know who *she* is? Or, more likely, was?"

"Somebody famous enough to have a museum," Addie said wearily.

"This is Elmwood, Nebraska," Loch said. "How much is that saying?"

Burke snorted. "Come on. I'm hoping I can find a pair of shoes—and maybe some real pants. This just looks weird," he said, gesturing at the dress shoes he was wearing with his sweatpants. There hadn't been much at the silo in his size—at least the rest of them had sneakers.

It seemed bizarrely anticlimactic to take time out from worrying about the fate of the world to go shopping, but Vivian had pointed out that the more they moved around, the more likely it was they'd manage to run into the Hallows. And she said she wanted to see what she could find out about Breakthrough and Radial using someone else's ISP, which meant a trip to the local library or some other WiFi hotspot.

"And I'd like to find something that makes me look less like a Hallmark Christmas Special," Addie said, wrinkling her nose.

"Or a very special episode of *What Not To Wear*," Loch said helpfully.

Spirit met Addie's gaze. *Underwear*, she mouthed silently, and Addie nodded vigorously. "Hey, we've got fifty bucks," she said, striving to sound cheerful "We can come up with whole wardrobes for that—and besides, I can sew, remember?"

"And whatever it is, it won't be gold, brown, or cream," Addie said feelingly.

※

Addie and Loch looked completely baffled as they followed Spirit and Burke through the store. *Well why not?* Spirit thought. *Addie's heir to a billion-dollar pharmaceutical company. Loch's father did something that left Loch with a fat trust fund.* She doubted either one had seen the inside of a Goodwill Store—or any other thrift shop—in their lives, while the White family had shopped at them as a matter of course.

Taking pity on them, she led Loch and Burke to the racks of men's clothing. There weren't any jeans in Burke's size, but there were a pair of work pants in good condition. The real find was work boots in his size. They were battered and worn, but they'd certainly last as long as . . .

. . . *as long as we have to live if we don't win,* Spirit thought. Every time she managed to stop thinking about Mordred and the Apocalypse, something happened to remind her.

She left Loch and Burke browsing through shirts and went off with Addie.

"You're really good at this," Addie said, watching Spirit swiftly sort an entire box of underwear into two piles: possible purchases and totally hopeless.

"Not everybody's born rich," Spirit said absently. A moment later she heard her own words and turned to Addie in horror. "I'm so sorry! I didn't mean—"

Addie smiled ruefully. "It's okay. Really. I know I've led a pretty sheltered life. The way Oakhurst was run—not the magic and the craziness, but the uniforms and the rules about what you could have—covered up a lot of the distinctions between—"

"The haves and the have-nots?" Spirit asked with a smile.

"The haves and the have-even-mores," Addie corrected. "In my old life, I would never even have met someone like Loch, or—" she broke off suddenly, her face twisting with grief. "Or Muirin," she whispered. "I would never have met Muirin."

"She—" Spirit said. She stopped, shaking her head. It was too soon. "Come on," she said, "let's see if we can find tops that don't suck this much."

There wasn't a huge selection, but Spirit found a couple of long-sleeved T-shirts and a couple of heavyweight shirts to go over them. The shirts were plaid flannel, but at least they weren't *gross*. Since they were still under budget, she grabbed a couple of the nightgowns. The ones in the best condition were circus tent huge, but she could cut them down later.

If there *was* a later.

"Okay," she said, "Let's grab the guys and get out of here."

"Unless you want to see if the— The *you-know-whats* are here," Addie said with a faint smirk.

"Sure," Spirit said mockingly. "Probably in with the small appliances, right?"

When they found Burke and Loch, they were at the back of the store, in what seemed to be the "General Junk" department. Burke had a copy of *Huckleberry Finn* in his hand, frowning faintly at it. Loch was looking through a stack of Archie Comics.

Behind the two long tables of unloved books and magazines was a collection of battered cardboard boxes, some stacked precariously against the wall, some propped against the legs of the tables, some open on the floor. It was clear the boxes had once contained donations, and now had been used to consolidate the discards. A sign taped to the cinderblock wall behind them said "Fifty Cents Each."

As they approached, Loch dropped the comics back to the table. "I think I've found where Yard Sale rejects go to die," he said, and gestured toward the boxes.

"You'd be surprised at what people will waste good money on," Burke said absently, setting the book down and bending down to look into the nearest box of discards.

"I wonder if that's per item or for a whole box," Loch said, indicating the sign, "because if it's per box it's definitely a bargain. . . ." He walked over to a stack of battered boxes and pulled out a VCR tape. "If you're an archaeologist, of course."

"Burke?" Spirit said quietly. She was sick with sudden fear. He didn't look right. He didn't look right *at all.* Something was happening. Something that shouldn't be.

Loch looked up sharply at the sound of her voice. She saw the movement out of the corner of her eye, and wanted to say something—anything—but she couldn't look away from Burke. He'd gone utterly still. Not like waiting, or even like holding as still as you could and trying not to be noticed. Burke was as still as if he'd been turned to stone. She couldn't even see him breathe.

Loch didn't seem to notice either the strangeness of Burke's immobility or Spirit's sudden panic. He walked over and waved his hand back and forth in front of Burke's face jokingly. "Helllooooooo?"

"No. Wait," Spirit said in a small airless voice. But even as she spoke, Loch poked Burke in the chest with a careless finger—and froze into the same stillness.

"Loch!" Addie cried.

She dropped her armload of clothes to the ground. Spirit grabbed for her, but Addie was already moving. Spirit lunged after her, and this time got a good grip.

But Addie had already touched Loch.

And suddenly Spirit was . . . somewhere else.

*

It was almost as if she'd been suddenly blinded, though all around her was the gelid grey light of a rainy afternoon. She could see her body, but there was nothing else.

"Hello? Loch? Addie? Burke? Hello?"

No answer. Her friends were gone. The store was gone. Even the sounds and smells of the real world were gone. She stood in a formless grey space.

Just as she formed that thought the grayness swirled and parted as if it really was fog. She had no time to wonder who was responsible—was this an attack or just some weird new consequence of having magic?—when she realized she was staring at her bedroom.

Her *real* bedroom. The one in the house in Indiana, the one that was gone the way her whole family was gone. There was a poster on the wall for the third *Pirates of the Caribbean* movie, the one that had come out when she was thirteen, it had only survived a couple of months, because Fee's birthday was in August. . . .

As if the memory had possessed some sort of force, suddenly Spirit wasn't looking at it from a distance. She was standing in the middle of her bedroom—her bedroom as it had been four years ago. She saw a scattering of DVDs on the bedspread of Fee's bed. The moment she saw them, Spirit's cheeks flushed hot with shame, and she could hear—*really* hear, not just remember—the sound of Fee's voice. . . .

"She ruined them! She ruined all of them!"

"She stole my lace blouse—the one I worked on for weeks! She ruined it!" Now it was her own voice, filled with fury and self justification. For Fee's tenth birthday, Mom and Dad had gotten her DVDs of her favorite movies. All secondhand, but all in good condition. Fee had been thrilled, and all Spirit could think of, seeing her happiness, was how the day before, Fee had "borrowed" the lace tunic Spirit had spent weeks making, and climbed a tree and fell out and tore it to shreds.

And so she'd taken a pair of scissors and scratched each one of the disks, ruining them.

"Who are you? Why is this happening?" she shouted, while inside her mind she cried: *I'm sorry! I'm sorry, Fee! I didn't mean to hurt you like that—*

But the room melted away around her as if it were fog, and something new began to take shape. . . .

She turned and ran, holding her hands out in front of her in the hope she'd feel any obstacle instead of running into it.

There was nothing in front of her, nothing beneath her feet but flat smoothness. The mist swirled in front of her. She staggered to a stop, backing away slowly as the mist parted again to show. . . .

Her bedroom again. Early evening on a cold dark spring night. There was a wide red stripe of tape on the floor, marking her side of the room separate from Fee's. She'd been five when Fee's crib was moved into her room; she'd demanded the boundary line. Over the years it had gotten frayed, and she'd pulled it up one year and didn't bother to replace it. But it had still been there when she was eight.

When she was eight. . . .

"No, no, no!" she screamed. She didn't want to see this. She didn't want to *remember* this.

But suddenly she was standing in the empty room, hearing the frantic barking coming from outside. . . .

When she was eight, they'd had a dog named Mister Wiggle, a stray who just showed up one day. He was terrified of storms. He'd been outside one day when it started to thunder. Dad was in his studio, Mom was out, Fee was spending the night with friends. Spirit was the only one who heard him, and she was curled up in bed with a book, warm and comfortable. So she'd ignored the frantic barking until it stopped.

And they never saw Mister Wiggle again.

"I'm sorry!" she shouted. Tears were running down her face now. *"I didn't know you'd run away! You must have been so afraid. . . ."*

She turned and ran again, this time with her eyes closed,

running as fast as she could. She ran for long enough that if she'd been in the real world she'd have left the store, crossed the parking lot, the street, run for block after block. At last she was forced to stop, panting, winded, gasping for breath.

And as soon as she opened her eyes, the mist before her swirled and changed again, forcing her to remember—to relive—the scene it showed.

Flat Rock Elementary School. Her fifth grade classroom. She'd had Mrs. Beech.

Flat Rock Indiana was the closest town to where they'd lived, and it was where she'd gone to school until eighth grade—the high school was a two-hour bus ride from home, and Dad had been fighting with the school board anyway, so after that she'd been homeschooled. But she'd gone to school in Flat Rock until she was twelve.

She looked around the empty classroom. She could hear the whisper of children, the scrape of chalk on the blackboard.

"Stop it!" she yelled.

But she could hear Mrs. Beech announcing the test, and heard the rustle and shuffle of papers as the tests were handed out. It was a math test. And she'd cheated.

She'd known the answers—she was good at math—but she was bored and didn't want to go to the trouble of solving the problems. So she'd cheated. And accused the boy she'd copied from of being the cheater. And gotten away with it. . . .

"Yes!" she shouted, as the classroom dissolved and another image began to form. *"Yes, I did those things! All of them! But they*

were wrong! And I was sorry! That's not all I am! That's not who I am!"

She didn't know why she was being forced to relive all her worst moments—not the bad things that had happened to her, but the bad things she'd done: every time she'd been mean, or cruel, or selfish; every time she'd disappointed Mom, or Dad—or herself. She knew they were being dragged out of her memories, and each one was more horrible than the last. There seemed to be no end to them. She knew—somehow— that they'd continue until she broke under the weight of her guilt and her shame.

And who would stop Mordred then?

She had to fight back.

How?

That's not all I am! That's not who I am!

Then prove it.

The second voice, the second thought, seemed to be her and not-her, and for an instant Spirit thought of the woman she'd glimpsed in her dream. But she had no time to trace that thought to its source. The mist was parting again. She could smell the smoke of an autumn bonfire. . . .

She closed her eyes and concentrated, summoning a different memory.

She was standing in her bedroom, looking at the shredded paper that covered the floor. Her posters. All the books she'd saved up her money to buy. . . .

Fee had torn them all to shreds, even though Spirit had

confessed about the DVDs and apologized. And when she'd gone back to her room afterward, this was what she'd found. She'd cleaned up the mess and never said a word about it. And she replaced every one of Fee's birthday presents, even though it took all her allowance for the next six months.

She still smelled the bonfire, and felt the cold October wind. She summoned another memory.

Jayce Bingham at school, showing off his new cell phone, something Spirit could never hope to own. Annie Morgan was looking at her sympathetically. Spirit knew Annie thought she had a hard life. She sympathized with Spirit every time something like this happened. It would have been easy for Spirit to agree, to complain about her parents forcing her to live in the Dark Ages: no cable, no cell phone, no iPod, and only dial-up at home. Secondhand clothes. Her parents' weird hippie friends.

She never did, no matter how tempting it was.

Was the wind dying down? Was the smell of burning leaves fainter? She didn't dare open her eyes to check.

She remembered the night she *hadn't* gone to the eighth grade dance. Davey Logan had asked her, but there'd been no money in the budget for a prom dress, or even for the fabric to make one, so she'd turned him down. Dad had known she was disappointed. He'd cajoled her into making fudge—a special treat. And while the pans were cooling, he'd asked her what she'd think about doing high school at home.

She'd hated the thought. *I'll be buried alive and never see any-*

body! But he'd looked at her hopefully, and she knew it was what he wanted for her, so she took a deep breath, and forced herself to smile, and said it would be great.

She thought of every time she'd been proud of herself, even if it was a secret she never told. When she'd seen what she should do—honesty, kindness, perseverance, keeping her word—and done it for no other reason than it was right.

She didn't give up in the hospital, or in rehab, even though it hurt and she hated it and she didn't see any point.

At Oakhurst, she didn't give in to being who they were trying to turn her into. She was scared and confused, but she kept trying to do the right thing, not the easy thing.

Even when it looked like the right thing would just get her killed.

She was scared, but she'd faced the Demon Lord of Hell, even though she'd been so terrified she could hardly stand up. Because it was the right thing to do. And this was an even bigger fight, and she didn't think she was the right person for it—that any of them were—and it would even look like being smart to try to get to Addie's trustees for help instead of trying to do this themselves. Nobody would blame her if she said she'd changed her mind.

But it would be wrong. This is our fight, and I have to stop telling myself nobody expects me to be a hero. It doesn't matter if I don't think I'm a hero, either. I'm going to do everything I can, no matter what it is.

"Do you hear me?" she shouted. *"I don't care what you do! I'm*

*not giving up! I may not be Oakhurst's definition of a winner, but
I'm not what you're trying to say I am! I won't give up! I won't!"*

Suddenly a Voice sounded in her ears: stern, kind, loving,
severe. Merciful and unforgiving, filled with a thousand con-
tradictions.

*"You have been found worthy, you will be consecrated for the
Hallows."*

She opened her eyes in surprise—the grey space was gone,
she was surrounded by golden light, and warmth, and she could
smell flowers. And just like that—before she could really think
about it—she was standing next to Burke, blinking at the harsh
fluorescent lights.

"You kids want that box, you can have the whole thing for
a buck."

They all jumped at the sound of the floorwalker's voice.
The woman stared at them with a tired, suspicious look.

"Uh . . . yeah," Burke said. "We'll take it."

"And those," Addie said quickly, as the floorwalker turned
to pick up the things she'd dropped. "Those too."

THREE

I'd been hoping there'd be something in there you'd like. You know, just a little thing. I knew you blamed yourself for . . . for what happened to Muirin, and for not telling us about Merlin. . . ." Burke said slowly. "I knew you'd done right, and done all you could, and you couldn't see it. I wanted to cheer you up. And then . . . I was in a place that was all grey, and . . . I saw every time I'd ever used my size, my strength, to get my own way. No. Worse than that. To bully somebody because I knew they could never fight back. To get what I wanted because they were afraid of me. To hurt someone just because I could."

They were sitting in the back of the van, all four of them, with the box between them. It was a little crowded, because the space right behind the seats was filled with bags from their earlier trip to the grocery.

"Me, too," Loch said quietly. "Not bullying. Not that way. But manipulating people. So they'd look like they were in the wrong, even though I'd pushed them into doing. . . . I saw all of it. I saw all the times I just turned my back on something I knew was wrong, because I wasn't willing to fight for what I knew was right."

"I just. . . ." Addie raised her hands, and let them fall into her lap again. "I don't know what to say. I saw . . . every time I just *went along* with things. Everybody else seemed to know what I should do, and . . . even when I didn't think they were right, I just went along with it. And . . . that's okay when you're five. But I knew I could spend the rest of my life just doing what I was told. And never doing anything that mattered. And I don't want that!" she finished fiercely. "I want . . . I want to make my own mistakes!"

Spirit reached out and took her hand. Addie squeezed it gratefully.

Loch opened his mouth to say something, then closed it again, looking thoughtful.

Spirit had gone first, telling them what had happened—or what she thought had happened. She wasn't really surprised to hear the same thing had happened to all of them. "But you all found a way to— To fight back, right? To tell the, the whatever-it-was that what it showed you might be true, but it wasn't the whole truth," Spirit said.

"I heard an angel speak to me," Burke said solemnly. "I prayed for strength and guidance, and it said I was worthy." He looked sheepish and awestruck at the same time.

"Worthy to be consecrated to the Hallows," Loch said softly, nodding. They'd all heard the same words at the end. "I don't know if it was an angel or not, but . . . it was something big. Something powerful. And it wanted to know that I understood the difference between right and wrong and to know that when I'd done wrong, I turned around and made up for it. It wanted to know if I . . . I don't know . . . was *mature* enough to say that since we *know* we're the only hope Merlin has, that I wouldn't let him down." He sighed. "I don't like fighting. I've always run away, and when I couldn't run any more, well, things never went that well. But I'm not going to run. And I'm going to fight."

"Me, too," Spirit said.

"And I—I'm going to stop being *nice*," Addie said firmly. "Um, well, *you* know," she added awkwardly.

Everyone laughed. Loch nudged her and grinned. "'She is intolerable curst, And shrewd and froward,'" he quoted (it was Shakespeare), and Addie stuck her tongue out at him.

"So . . . where are these 'Hallows' we're all worthy of?" Spirit asked. The box that had started all this was too small to hold a cauldron, let alone a sword or a spear.

"Here," Addie said. She dug around in the box for a moment, and withdrew a set of car keys. The tag was a battered old GM logo on a plain steel split ring with a set of worn keys. But somehow—Spirit blinked as she looked at them—they were more *real* than anything else around them. "This one's mine. I don't know what it has to do with a cauldron or cup, but I know it's mine. Your turn," she said, nodding to Loch.

70

Loch approached the box much more tentatively than Addie had, as if he suspected whatever was in there might bite. He picked through it gingerly. Spirit saw a couple of refrigerator magnets, a battered deck of playing cards, some poker chips, a litter of pens and pencils, plastic Mardi Gras necklaces, worn action figures, six-sided dice. . . . Nothing but junk. Finally Loch plucked out something too small to see.

"Phone charm," he said, holding it out on the palm of his hand.

It was a tiny plastic arrowhead, no longer than his thumbnail, with the usual long loop of cord to attach it to a cell phone. "Presenting . . . the Spear. Fitting, I suppose, given my name," he added. "Although if I'm going to use it, I may need a slingshot. Now you," he said to Spirit.

"No, I. . . . Could. . . . Burke, could you?" Despite her vow in the grey space, despite having been pronounced "worthy" by whatever the Voice had been (Burke said it was an angel, but Spirit lacked his easy faith), she felt strangely reluctant to find out which Hallow was going to be hers.

"Sure," Burke said, smiling. He rooted around in the box for longer than either of the others had, and finally came up with one of the pens. It was a cheap ballpoint, the kind businesses used to give out, but whatever name had been on the white plastic body had been worn away. He held it for a long moment, then frowned. "I think this is yours, not mine," he said, offering it to Spirit. She took it automatically. As she did, there was a single bright flash in her mind, and she knew Burke had

71

been right. This was the Sword. This was hers. She knew that beyond doubt.

What she didn't know was how to turn the pen *into* the Sword, if that was what she was supposed to do. She stared down at it in puzzlement.

"Well? What is it? Or which is it, I should say?" Addie demanded.

"It's the Sword." It was Burke who answered. He held up his prize. "Because I have the Shield, so that makes all four."

The Shield Hallow of Britain was a set of men's rings tied together with a scrap of pink yarn. They were both cheap pot-metal, with a gold plating that was mostly worn off. Their squared tops had symbols on them, picked out in rhinestones that were miraculously all still there: one an ace, and one a diamond.

You're nothing but a pack of cards, Spirit thought giddily.

"Well, that was . . . suspiciously easy," Loch said, sounding puzzled.

"Nice that *something* is," Addie grumbled.

"Anybody want the rest of this stuff?" Burke asked, nodding toward the box.

"Not unless there's a large, well-equipped army in there somewhere," Loch said. He poked at the box hopefully. "I don't suppose any of you action figures come to life when I call you? No? Right then."

Burke nodded again and opened the back door. He climbed out with the box and set it on the ground next to the nearest garbage can.

"Anybody feel any different?" he asked when he came back. Spirit saw the others shake their heads. She shrugged. Except for *knowing* the object she held was the Sword Hallow, nothing was any different.

Burke climbed back in and pulled the door shut. "Well, maybe later," he said. "At least we found them."

Spirit couldn't figure out quite how she felt. Finding the Hallows seemed almost like an anticlimax. And yet . . . it also felt like it was the *beginning* of something, as if this was right before a tornado, and she had looked up and the sky was turning green.

"Yeah," Loch said. "Too bad Vivian didn't mention the booby trap." He made a face. "It's a good thing nobody noticed us playing statues back there, or we could have found ourselves locked up or something."

"Maybe she didn't know," Spirit said. "But . . . imagine what would have happened to Mark if he'd found them? Or Teddy? Or Madison?" She thought about that. She kind of wished it could have happened.

Clearly, so did Loch. "Or Ovcharenko," Loch said with a dark smile. "Too bad there's no way to know. I'd pay real money to watch."

"I think we can guess, though," Spirit said. "It wasn't a booby trap, not really. It was a test. Of worthiness. The grey place turned all our best qualities inside out. It showed us our dark sides, to see if we could rise above them—or *had* risen above them, ever. And, you know, that makes me wonder— now that we've all seen that—why does anyone become a

Shadow Knight? Or really, *stay* a Shadow Knight once they know what's involved besides fancy limousines and penthouses, or whatever they get? Because—oh, I don't know!"

"I do," Addie said. "Who wants to be the bad guy, knowing they're the bad guy? I mean, usually there's a certain amount of . . . rationalization going on in the mind of your average supervillain. You know."

"So to speak," Loch said. "But yeah. The whole 'this hurts me more than it hurts you' thing. My— My father said once that the secret to success in business was knowing that nobody is the villain in their own story. And this isn't exactly that, but. . . ."

"Some people just like knowing they can always get their own way," Burke said quietly. "They don't think about other people enough to care what they're feeling."

Loch frowned. "Actually . . . some people just can't see other people as anything other than props. There were more than a couple of CEOs like that. They'd laugh about firing people, as if other people just weren't real to them. Then they'd run out and drop five hundred bucks on dinner. Maybe that's it. Maybe in order to be a Shadow Knight—everyone *else* is a shadow to you."

Burke nodded. "So, nobody else matters because nobody else has feelings or importance except you. No reason why you can't just shove them around, since they're just extras in *your* play."

"That isn't you," Spirit said firmly, meeting and holding his gaze. After a moment he smiled ruefully in acknowledgment.

"But," she added, turning to include the others, "are we going to be immune? I mean, we beat it once, but if someone—Mordred—offers us—"

"The kingdoms of the Earth," Burke said.

"Right," Loch said. "Come to the Dark Side! Not only are there cookies, but there's safety and luxury and peasants to torture!"

"If that's the sort of thing you want," Addie said dryly. Loch made a rude noise and shook his head.

"We've just got to hope we'll be smart when the time comes," Burke said. "Or. . . . I dunno . . . *valiant*. And now we'd better get a move on. Because I don't think keeping Vivian waiting is real smart either."

⁂

The house-turned-museum was an old square two-story building that Loch instantly dubbed a "house kind of a house" on a back street. They pulled up and Burke went inside to see if Vivian was there and returned with a handful of pamphlets. Bess Streeter Aldrich turned out to be an author none of them had ever heard of, who'd published her last book around the time their grandparents probably started dating. About fifteen minutes later, Vivian showed up on her bike. Burke jumped out and opened the back so she could load it in.

"Anything?" he asked.

"Not here," she said briefly, tossing her backpack in after the bike. She walked up to the driver's side and opened the door, holding out her hand for the keys.

"I can drive," Loch protested.

"And *I* have an actual license," Vivian said. Loch shrugged and got out.

They stopped on the way back at a roadside hamburger stand—a kind of freelance McDonald's—for lunch. There were no other customers, no drive-through, and no carhops. They had to walk up to the window themselves to get served. Nobody talked much. Vivian wasn't the type to encourage conversation, and for their parts, Spirit and her friends were still freaked by the idea they now had ancient magic artifacts of mysterious (but vague) power in their possession. When they got back to the silo—Spirit could tell from Loch's expression that Vivian had taken a different route this time—they all pitched in to bring the stuff down below. By the time they had it stowed away, every cupboard in the tiny kitchen was stuffed.

"Looks like we won't have to go shopping for a while," Burke said mildly.

Vivian smiled darkly. "Not unless you want fresh milk, but I figure you're going to be running around trying to scare up the Hallows. You're on a deadline, you know."

Addie looked at Spirit. Loch glanced from the two of them to Burke. There was a moment of guilty silence.

"You really can't tell whether or not we have them?" Spirit asked carefully. "Because we do. We found them today."

Vivian's shock was genuine. She sucked in a sharp breath and leaned back against the counter, gripping the edge tightly. "Holy Epona be praised that the Great Hallows are safe again," she said. "It's true?" she added sharply. "You're telling the truth?"

"It would be a pretty stupid thing to lie about," Loch said tartly. "Here—see?" He held out the phone charm on his palm. "I know it doesn't look like much, but—"

"It's the Spear," Vivian said. She closed her eyes for a moment, and Spirit thought she saw a glitter of tears. "I. . . . I've hoped for so long. . . ." She turned around to face the cabinets and took another deep breath, clearly trying to compose herself. "That makes this easier," she said.

"Makes what easier?" Spirit asked, trying not to sound as apprehensive as she felt. Vivian was certainly on their side, but Spirit suspected she was telling them as little as possible.

"I have to go away. I'm leaving in the morning. I may not be back. *Ever.*"

"What?" Burke said. "Why? Where?"

"To perform a task—if I can. But you don't need me any longer. The next part in this is yours, not mine. I have always known that."

"But— Can't we help you? With . . . whatever-it-is?" Spirit asked.

Vivian just shook her head.

"Isn't there anything you can tell us?" Addie pleaded. "We've found the Hallows, but we don't know how to use them. We can't even turn them into what they're supposed to be."

"The Hallows themselves will instruct you," Vivian said, still sounding a little rattled. She turned around to face them again. "You must have faith. Truly. Ask Merlin, and he will tell you the same. The Hallows will show you the way."

"But—" Loch said.

"No," Spirit said firmly, somehow *sure* that Vivian was right, and that this was the way things had to be. She didn't know where this sense of certainty was coming from, but she knew it was true so solidly that it was as if it had always been true. "This is up to us now. If Vivian could've stopped Mordred, she would have. If she knew how—or . . . anything— she'd tell us."

Vivian smiled at Spirit with genuine warmth. "Got it in one, kid. Good luck with heading off the Apocalypse."

"Thanks—I think," Spirit said ruefully.

"Can't you even tell us which Reincarnates we are, and how we get our memories back?" Loch asked. "Oh, come on," he said, looking at the others, "anybody who didn't figure we had to be Reincarnates to find the Hallows hasn't been paying attention."

"You're right, my—my dear boy," Vivian said. Spirit had the feeling she'd changed what she was going to say in the middle. "But I'm not crazy enough to stick my nose into the middle of magic this powerful. You'll find out when you're meant to."

"This is like every bad teen slasher movie ever filmed," Loch complained. "You know things we need to know. And you won't tell us."

"Yes," Vivian said, sounding more like her usual exasperated self. "Because if I tell you before you *know,* you might never know at all. Things have to come in the right order, or nothing works. It's like a spell, only a lot more powerful than any spell you've ever been involved with before. You know how spells work. Do the steps out of order and you get nothing. Or something really bad. You've been hidden carefully—even from yourselves. If something goes wrong this time, you won't be reborn to try again. And Mordred wins. Forever."

Because Merlin will die, Spirit realized. Whether Mordred knew where—and what—Merlin was or not, when Mordred blew up the Internet, Merlin would be gone.

"Let it go, Loch. She's been right so far," Spirit said.

Loch waved his hand irritably—agreeing or arguing, Spirit couldn't tell—and stalked out of the kitchen.

"So . . . what should we do now?" Addie asked hesitantly.

The question startled Vivian into a sharp bark of laughter. "Do? Do anything you want. It's all up to the Hallows now, so do whatever you want to until they decide the time is right."

❧

Spirit wanted to talk to Merlin. They'd done the first thing they had to do, and she was hoping he might be more forthcoming than Vivian had been—or at least tell her what had to happen next. But she felt oddly shy about saying so. When the others agreed the best thing to do was try to figure out how to use the magical weapons they'd been given, Spirit went along with it. She suspected none of them wanted to admit to the others that they were afraid that mastering their Hallow would awaken their Reincarnate memories. Becoming someone else—*remembering* being someone else—seemed like amnesia-in-reverse. Or dying.

But if they hadn't been willing to die, they would all have

gone along with Mordred. Of all the people at Oakhurst, at Breakthrough, or in Radial, they, the five of them (because it had been Muirin's choice, too), were the only ones who had a true understanding of the choice they'd be making: join Mordred as his favored sorcerous henchmen in a post-Apocalyptic wilderness, or . . .

. . . or do exactly what they were doing now, and fight back any way they could.

No matter the cost.

Since none of them had really destructive Gifts—not like Van Cartwright or some of the other Fire Witches or Weather Witches they all knew—by unspoken agreement they designated the rec room next to the bedroom as a sort of practice room. There, one by one, they sat trying to figure out how to use—or even just *activate*—the magical weapons they'd been given.

Burke, of course, went first.

❧

With nothing else to do while the others were practicing— Spirit had asked to go last—and with the prospect of Vivian deserting them looming on the horizon, Spirit decided to ask Vivian to show her how the computer console worked. It was the only way for her to talk to Merlin, and she wanted to be sure she'd be able to.

Vivian walked Spirit through the procedure for powering up the huge old computer. It ran on tubes, not chips, Vivian told her, so she couldn't just flip a switch and expect it to start immediately. And once the system had power, there would be another long wait while the system—a modem dialing out over telephone lines—could make its connection to the Internet.

"Can I ask you a question?" Spirit asked, waiting for the amber lights on the console to go green.

"You can *ask*," Vivian said cautiously.

"It's about my— My Gift," Spirit said hesitantly. "You were at Oakhurst a long time ago, right?"

"Don't make it sound like it was sometime in the last century," Vivian said. "Oh . . . *wait*. . . ."

Spirit smiled faintly at the tiny joke. "I just wondered . . . did they teach the Fifth School when you were there? Doc— One of the staff there had heard of it, but. . . ."

Vivian looked sympathetic. "I'm sorry, Spirit. Ms. Groves talked about it a little, but she said Spirit Mages were so rare, there was no point in teaching that School."

"That doesn't sound . . . like her," Spirit said, swallowing against the lump in her throat.

"She's dead, isn't she?" Vivian asked quietly.

Spirit nodded, unable to speak.

"I'm sorry. She was a holy terror, but she never played the games a lot of the staff did. And you're right. It *doesn't* make sense. They taught all of us about all the Schools, no matter what our Gift was. Why not that one?"

"I don't know," Spirit said, scrubbing at her eyes angrily. She was tired of crying. And she was tired of people dying, too. "It's like they all just . . . *forgot*, or something."

Vivian nodded soberly. "There was a lot of that going around, and not just the students. Stuff like some of the teachers just forgetting about the kids who disappeared, not even *trying* to track them down, even when the kid had been someone they were trying to give extra attention to."

Yeah. And three guesses who did that.

Spirit wondered why Mordred had been trying to cover up the existence of the Fifth School. It would have been so much easier to deny it even existed. How would the students know?

And that meant . . . the School of Spirit was important.

Important enough to bring Mordred down?

That would sure have been a good reason to keep anyone from finding out about it.

Her thoughts were interrupted by the hiss of static over the speakers—an indication of an open phone line—followed by the "bong bong" sound that Vivian called a "handshake." It meant their system had made a connection.

"That's it," Vivian said. "You're live. I've still got some stuff to do before I leave, so I'll leave you two to chat. Be sure to shut the system down when you're done using it. If anything breaks, you'll need to build a time machine before you can order parts."

"I won't forget," Spirit said.

Vivian left the control bunker, and Spirit took a deep breath, watching the square green cursor pulse hypnotically on the little screen.

HELLO, QUERCUS, she typed. OR SHOULD I CALL YOU MERLIN? It was an effort to hit each key hard enough to activate it, and her fingers were starting to ache already.

YOU MAY CALL ME WHAT YOU WISH, SPIRIT. The letters formed one by one on the screen. Spirit didn't know if the slowness was due to the ancient technology they were using, or the fact that Merlin was thinking carefully about each word.

VIVIAN CALLS YOU MERLIN, SO I WILL TOO. SHE'S LEAVING TOMORROW. SHE WON'T SAY WHERE SHE'S GOING. BUT

Spirit's fingers hovered over the keyboard indecisively. She trusted Merlin completely, but she wasn't sure whether she should talk about the Hallows. What if someone was eavesdropping?

SPIRIT? YOU MAY SAY ANYTHING YOU WISH TO WITHOUT FEAR. IF IT WERE POSSIBLE FOR OUR ENEMIES TO FIND ME, I WOULD HAVE BEEN DESTROYED LONG AGO.

Spirit released a deep breath she hadn't known she was holding. WE FOUND THE HALLOWS, she typed. BUT THEY DON'T WORK. I MEAN, WE CAN'T MAKE THEM DO ANYTHING.

BUT YOU WERE CONSECRATED TO THE HALLOWS, came the response. Spirit wasn't sure whether it was a question or not.

YES, she typed back.

THEN HAVE PATIENCE AND FAITH. ALL WILL BE WELL.

HOW CAN YOU BE SURE OF THAT? The keyboard was too slow for her to type all the things in her mind: how was patience going to stop Mordred? How could she—how could any of them—have faith that they could defeat Mordred? How could they have faith in the power of the Hallows when they couldn't even make them *work?*

I AM A VERY OLD MAN. (Spirit could almost hear the wry chuckle accompanying those words.) I HAVE HAD TIME TO LEARN THE POWER OF FAITH. AND OF TRUST.

HOW CAN YOU TRUST US? Spirit answered. YOU DON'T EVEN KNOW US.

I HAVE KNOWN YOU LONGER THAN YOU IMAGINE, SPIRIT WHITE. BELIEVE IN YOURSELF.

That was so close to one of those irritating catchphrases from Oakhurst's Morning Motivational Messages that Spirit couldn't keep herself from making a face. She was instantly ashamed of herself—just because Oakhurst had done its best to pervert everything good and kind and normal was no reason she should buy into their lies.

I'LL TRY, she answered.

✦

By the time Spirit's turn to try out her Hallow came, none of the others had been able to announce any success in activating theirs. Spirit sat down at the table and set the pen in front of her. She stared at it gloomily. The pen just sat there.

The pen was . . . just a pen. It was clearly magical—it had the same numinous hyper-reality Addie's car keys possessed, or Loch's phone charm, or Burke's tacky jewelry—but aside from that. . . .

Nothing.

This entire exercise reminded Spirit far too much of her first days at Oakhurst, when Miss Smith had locked her up in a room with a potted plant, a bowl of water, a candle, and a bundle of feathers, and told her to figure out which Elemental School her Gift belonged to. It hadn't worked then, and it didn't work now.

When she found herself absently tapping the pen against the table out of sheer boredom, Spirit gave up. If the mystic ballpoint was going to reveal its secret life as an enchanted sword, it wasn't going to do it this afternoon. Somehow, the fact that none of the others had had any better luck made Spirit feel better than it should have. She'd worried that their experience with their Gifts would make a difference, but . . . no.

At least this is one of those situations where prior experience doesn't count, she told herself. *Although with the fate of the world hanging in the balance, it might be nice if it did.*

She sighed as she got to her feet. Time to go tell Burke, Loch, and Addie that they were four for four in the "not activating the Hallows" department.

✦

Since tomorrow they'd be on their own, Burke and Spirit made dinner as a sort of practice run. Loch had said he was great at ordering room service, and Addie swore she'd never seen a kitchen in her life, so Spirit and Burke decided it was up to them to stave off group starvation after Vivian left. They were all trying hard to pretend this was just a sort of impromptu camping trip, something they might have done in the regular course of things. It didn't work very well, but it helped. After dinner, Vivian took all four of them on a tour of the bunker, showing them where all the switches and valves were, and how to operate them. A lot of the original signs were still up from when the bunker had been in use, and a lot of those were detailed directions, so that helped. Spirit couldn't decide whether it was creepy or kitschy. She wondered *why* there were such detailed directions, but . . . if someone was down here during a war, they might be hurt, sick with radiation. . . . Maybe that was why.

After that, the five of them went up to the surface. It was already dark, but the wind wasn't quite as cold as Spirit expected it to be. Spring was coming.

Maybe.

If they were lucky.

Vivian walked them around the area encompassed by the Wards. It was larger than Spirit had expected—easily several acres. Like the ones surrounding Oakhurst, the Wards were set at the cardinal points of the compass: north, south, east, and west. Burke had marked where he thought the bounds were on the ground with chalk. He'd been pretty close.

"You should re-cast them as often as possible," Vivian said. "I'll show you. Burke, come here."

Burke obediently came to stand beside her.

"This is the southern Ward, so it resonates most strongly to the Element of Earth. The Shield Hallow belongs to that element. Can you feel it?"

"Maybe," Burke said doubtfully. "I'm a Combat Mage. It's not like I've ever cast a spell."

"Sure you can," Vivian said patiently. "It's cold out here tonight, but there's one spot that feels warmer."

"Yes!" Burke exclaimed, sounding pleased. "Right here."

"Good. When you need to renew the Ward, take the Shield and hold it in that feeling of warmth. Concentrate on what you want."

"Protection," Burke said firmly, and Vivian made a sound of approval.

"But don't do it now," she added. "I need to be able to cross them later, not rip them to shreds."

"If we're powering the Wards up from the Hallows, won't that drain them?" Loch asked.

"They aren't flashlight batteries, rich boy," Vivian said. "They're— Well, you'll see. Or you won't. Anyway. You can use any of them at any of the anchor points, or the same one at all four, but it's strongest if you use each Hallow at its proper element. So the Cup in the West, the Spear in the North, and the Sword in the East."

"Earth, Water, Fire, and Air," Loch said. "Or in this case, I guess, Spirit."

"When was Oakhurst planning to teach us this stuff?" Addie asked crossly.

Vivian laughed at her disgruntled tone. "Probably never. They said you were all magicians and identified your Gifts, but Mordred certainly never intended to show you how to tap the power behind them. You can use that power for a lot more than water fights. Or not getting lost," she added, smirking at Loch.

"When we remember, will we know?" Spirit asked tentatively. Even though she was committed to this fight, the thought of waking up thinking she was somebody else frightened her more than she wanted to let on.

"You'll know that when you remember, won't you?" Vivian said, but her words lacked their usual bite.

I t hardly seems as if we've only been here a day and a half, Spirit thought, brushing her hair out as she got ready for bed. Yesterday morning they'd been on the road, fleeing from Oakhurst and the Shadow Knights. This morning they'd woken up here. Tomorrow morning, Vivian would be gone, and they'd be on their own again, with a deadline they had to beat and weapons they didn't know how to use.

"I'm not sure I'd wear a nightgown if I had one," Addie said, walking into the bunkroom. "It doesn't seem too cold during the day, but at night—*ooh!*"

"Well, I can always make the ones we bought into something else," Spirit said philosophically. "Shirts, maybe."

"Or I can heal our chilblains with these," Addie said, jingling the keys she now wore around her neck on a length of string. "If I ever figure them out."

"Good luck with that," Spirit said with a snort. The pen wasn't quite as convenient to carry, but she had it clipped to the neck of her sweatshirt. "Hey, Addie, do you suppose you got the Cauldron because you're a Water Witch?"

"I wondered about that," Addie said, "but no. Both Loch and Burke have Earth Gifts, and Loch has the Spear, which is a symbol of Fire. And you're not an Air Mage, but you have the Sword. . . ."

"Way to go, Addie," Spirit said. "Now I'm going to have nightmares all night wondering if only two of us are the right people to be doing this."

"Doing what?" Loch asked, walking in ahead of Burke. His pale blond hair was damp and slicked back, and like Addie, he was wearing his Hallow on a cord around his neck.

"Saving the world," Addie said.

"We hope," Loch said.

"We will," Burke said, with more confidence than Spirit felt. "Want me to turn the lights out?"

"As long as somebody has a flashlight," Spirit said.

Addie reached under her pillow and brandished the flashlight Vivian had been using earlier. Burke flipped the switch—it was on the wall outside the room—and suddenly the bunkroom was cave-dark.

"Hey," Loch said, aggrieved.

"Deal with it," Burke answered.

Spirit heard springs squeak as Loch climbed into the bunk above Addie, then felt her own bed shake as Burke climbed in above her. Then there was silence for a moment.

"You know," Addie said forlornly. "I never thought I'd miss *anything* about Oakhurst. But I miss my computer, even though all I could get was the school intranet. And *books.*"

"Yeah," Burke said. "If I'd been thinking, I would've picked up some of the ones at that Goodwill today."

"The world's going to end in a month and you're *bored?*" Loch asked.

"Ha ha very funny," Spirit said, deadpan. "I'm not going to miss being worked to death twenty-four seven."

"Or the Morning Motivational Message," Addie said.

"Or *Systema,*" Burke said.

"Oh, I'm *really* not going to miss *Systema,*" Loch said. "But what about our healthful cross-country horseback rides?"

Suddenly it became a game, as each of them contributed things they would *not* miss about Oakhurst: the dress code, the etiquette lessons, ballroom dancing, the compulsory sports, the curfews, the censorship. . . .

It helped chase away the things they didn't really want to think about. But what it did most was remind them how strange their current situation was.

FOUR

After the others fell silent, Spirit stayed awake as long as she could. Her friends were all asleep, but she dreaded the thought of sleeping. Of dreaming again.

What was it like when you remembered having been someone else? Was it like dying? Would she forget she'd ever been Spirit White and had a sister named Phoenix and parents who'd loved her? Would she forget everything that made her *her*? She didn't know. If it had been simple—if someone had come to her and said: "Step in front of this firing squad and the world will be safe"—she thought she could have managed to do that. But this was different. This was like dying and having to stick around afterward knowing you were dead.

Or like something even worse . . . if there *was* something worse.

If there was actually something worse than that, Spirit

couldn't even imagine it. With all the magic classes there'd been at Oakhurst, there hadn't been one single one dealing with waking up to find you were a reincarnation of somebody and the person you thought you were didn't actually exist.

Funny thing that. Only not.

She would have gotten up and gone out into the computer room—hung out with Merlin, or tried to see if she could get onto the actual Internet with the silo's antique equipment—but she knew if she went blundering around in the dark, she'd wake the others up. And then what could she say to explain?

I'll just stay awake until morning, she told herself. *Maybe I won't dream if I sleep during the day.*

I'll just stay awake.

✴

She was walking through an empty castle. It wasn't a castle like in Fee's movies, or like the castles you saw in drawings. It was smaller somehow. Instead of carpets on the stone floors, there was straw, and the carpets were hung on the walls. It wasn't all stone, either, like the ones in the movies. A lot of it was wood.

She didn't know how she'd gotten here, but she wasn't worried. As soon as she found what she was looking for, she'd go back.

Maybe it was in the stone tower. The tower was huge, both tall and wide, with wooden steps spiraling upward along the inside wall. The steps were thick planks of wood that seemed to have been set into the wall at the same time the wall had been built—she knew that without knowing how she knew. It would be centuries before the wood rotted away—if it ever did—and then the masons would take a new baulk of timber and hammer it into the empty hole, wedging it in as tight as its predecessor had been.

The castle had been built to endure.

The steps went up through an opening cut into each wooden floor. Nobody lived in this part of the castle—this was the siege tower, the place for a last stand, the place you went to when the castle was about to fall. Each chamber was filled with provisions—sacks of grain, barrels of salt fish and salt pork, barrels filled with arrows, chests filled with leather armor and coats of ring mail. Spirit counted as she climbed: one story, two stories, three stories, four, and still the stairs spiraled upward. She'd be able to see the entire world from the top.

The top floor was more window than wall, built around four tall stone pillars that held up the wood and thatch roof. She didn't envy the man who'd thatched it; he must have been very brave, or very drunk. The pillars had been plastered, covering the rough stone with a smooth white surface. The wooden floor had been whitened as well. She stepped away from the top of the staircase and peered out. She could see for miles—but when she looked down, the momentary illusion of peace was shattered.

There were two armies facing each other on the vast green meadow. The sunlight glittered off the armor of the men and the horses, and just ahead of the front rank of fighters on each side, there was a man on horseback carrying a banner. The wind whipped at the banners, unfurling them so she could see the designs. One was red, with a black dragon coiled around a black tower—

That's the Breakthrough logo. I recognize it.

—while the other banner was as blue as an October sky and showed a white horse. It glittered as the sunlight caught it; the horse had been stitched with threads of silver.

I know that design.

"Are you ready?" It was a woman's voice, speaking from behind her. "You can still turn back."

"No," Spirit answered sorrowfully. "I can't. I never could."

She turned around to see a woman dressed in chain mail and leather armor and wearing a sword. Spirit knew she'd seen her before. But this time the woman wasn't wearing a helmet, and Spirit could see her face.

It was like looking into a mirror.

"Then defend the light," the woman said. She stepped forward and kissed Spirit on the forehead. . . .

. . . and Spirit woke up.

⁕

She was Spirit White. She was Guinevere of Camelot. She remembered both lives. Ice cream and Sunday drives and growing up in Indiana. A castle on a mountaintop, riding and swordplay and learning to be a queen.

She remembered the day she rode out from her castle to meet the man her visions had told her she would marry.

She remembered the first time Burke had kissed her.

She sat up. The strange cage of metal shook, then a familiar figure stood before her. She smiled in delight and relief.

"Arthur! Husband!" *Oh my god,* Spirit thought in horror, clapping her hands over her mouth as she felt the heat rise in her cheeks.

"Aye," Burke said softly, and shook his head at the sound of his own voice. He was clearly as shaken as she was. He held out a hand and she grabbed it, using it to pull herself to her feet.

Loch—Addie—

She looked toward the other bunks. Loch was sitting up, staring around himself wildly as if he couldn't imagine how he'd gotten up there and had no idea of how to get down. *Ah, Lancelot. The most graceful man a-horse I have ever seen—and the clumsiest afoot.*

"No," Spirit said aloud.

"Yes!" Vivianne, The Lady of the Lake, sat on the edge of her bed, pushing her long black hair out of her eyes.

No! That's Addie!

"It's— The—" Addie/Vivianne said. She was both, just as Loch was Lachlan Spears and Lancelot of the Lake, as Spirit was also Guinevere. . . .

"My liege," Loch said, scrambling down from the top bunk. "Know that I am your sworn knight unto death." He started to kneel, then caught himself. "Uh . . . not that I'm, um, planning to *die. . . .*"

The weak joke broke the tension, and they all laughed.

95

"Well," Addie said, looking at Burke, "weren't we all wondering where Arthur was?" She looked down at the sweatshirt and sweatpants she was wearing with an unfeigned horror. *Well,* Spirit recalled, *Vivianne had always been one for fine robes and rich fabrics. . . .*

"Oh my god, I feel like I'm losing my mind," Addie and Spirit both said, practically in chorus.

"More like getting a second one," Burke said. He put an arm around Spirit. "My lady," he said softly, and Spirit couldn't tell whether it was Burke or the Reincarnate memories speaking.

"She knew," Spirit said in sudden realization. "Vivian—not you, Addie, *her*—she knew who we were."

"But how could she?" Addie demanded. "Her fell arts—sorry!—her magic couldn't have told her. Didn't Elizabeth say Reincarnates couldn't recognize each other unless *both* sides had their memories back?"

"Aye," Burke said. "But The Merlin never lost his. He knew all along. He has to have told her." He stepped away from Spirit and ran both hands through his hair, as if his head hurt.

"She said I should know her," Loch said. "She said Vivian was her real name."

"No," Addie said in a strange voice. "It was Nimue. We—They— There wasn't one Lady-of-the-Lake. There were three of us. Them. Vivianne, Ninniane, and Nimue."

The Lady of the Lake, Spirit suddenly remembered, had been Lancelot's foster mother. "And Nimue was seduced by Mordred, and betrayed Merlin," Spirit said.

She remembered the desperate weeks she'd spent hunting for the renegade priestess, for only she could undo the spell of imprisonment.

She remembered reading the story in one of her sister's books.

It was like being in an echo chamber. Every thought jarred a bunch of other thoughts loose, and she couldn't decide which was real. *Both?*

"The—" Loch said, and stopped, shaking his head. "This is just—" Suddenly, he looked horror-stricken. "Oh, god, do you know how many *people* I've killed?"

"Not you, Loch," Spirit said quickly. "Lancelot. He was a knight. He fought wars. It was . . . a more violent time. I've— I killed people, too." She remembered battlefields, and fighting beside Arthur, her sword in her hand. Her Reincarnate memories were starting to settle down, but knowing she was Guinevere with the same certainty she knew she was Spirit was hard to take.

"It's about to be a violent time *now*," Loch said, with a ghost of his old snark. "But—" He pulled the loop of cord off over his head and held the tiny charm up between his thumb and forefinger. "—at least I know what to do with this." There was a ripple of magic—and suddenly Loch was holding a full-sized war spear in his hands. Its head gleamed silver, and its entire length was banded in silver and painted with runes.

Spirit realized she was holding the pen in her hand. But it wasn't a pen. Partly that was illusion, partly it was a kind of talisman. The only way she could think of what she did next was as if the talisman were a sock and she were turning it inside out.

The sword she held in her hand was long and heavy. Letters too bright to see clearly danced down the length of the blade. The pommel was gold, inlaid with a design of the same white horse she'd seen on the banner.

On Guinevere's banner.

The others were all staring at her.

"Is that . . . Excalibur?" Loch asked. "Yes. It is," he said, answering himself. "I know that sword."

"Why do you have it if he's Arthur?" Addie asked. "Oh, and don't expect me to show off the Cauldron just yet. But I have a surprise for you later."

"Oh good, more surprises," Loch said unenthusiastically.

"She has it because it's hers," Burke said. "And because if I had it, I couldn't do . . . this."

He held both fists out in front of him. The cheap tacky rings glinted. Suddenly there was a silvery glow in the air in front of him. A shield.

"Unbreakable," Burke said with satisfaction. He lowered his hands and the shield-shape vanished. "This was what I truly should have been, back then. The protector. Maybe if I had been. . . ." he left that unfinished.

It only took a thought for Spirit to fold the Sword away again, and Loch had already done the same with the Spear. The four of them looked at each other.

"The legends got so much stuff wrong," Spirit said, because she knew now that it was Guinevere who'd given Arthur Excalibur, not The Lady of the Lake.

"The legend had it coming," Loch answered.

"So," Burke said, glancing at Spirit, "what now?"

"I know it sounds really stupid, but . . . I'm hungry," Addie said self-consciously.

"I can go out and—" Loch stopped, breaking off whatever he'd been about to say. "There's food in the kitchen. But it's going to be really weird having you guys do the cooking now."

"I—" Burke stopped. "Arthur didn't grow up in a fancy castle."

"That's not how Morgause tells it," Loch gibed.

"Kings and Queens or not," Spirit said, "unless Vivianne did her own cooking in Avalon, Burke and I are still your best hope to avoid starvation."

"Nope," Addie said with determined cheerfulness. "If there was a kitchen in Avalon, my other self never saw it."

＊

Almost two weeks had passed since Vivian's departure, and the four of them had settled into a routine. They worked harder than any of them—even Burke—had ever worked at Oakhurst, but now it was on one skill and for one goal.

Mastering the Hallows.

For Spirit and Loch, it was a matter of adapting lessons in armed combat they'd learned at Oakhurst to magical weapons: Excalibur and Arondight. Arondight—the Lance—would strike any target at which it was thrown, and Excalibur—the Sword—was said to give victory to whoever wielded it.

Burke's practice with the Shield was a little different, as he had to call it into being through an act of will, and its impenetrability was linked to his determination. Fortunately, Burke was very determined.

But it was Addie whose Hallow provided her with the greatest challange, for the Cauldron worked far differently from the other Hallows. Addie's keys didn't turn into anything, as the other tokens did, but when inserted into the ignition of any vehicle, they turned it into a Cauldron of Plenty, which could transform anything placed into it into whatever she wished it to become. The power of the Cauldron seemed—at first—to be infinite: magic without cost. But the need to place something into the Cauldron to transform it into something else meant that they couldn't simply, for example, wish up bombs or allies or something to strike Mordred and the Shadow Knights dead. Their victory would have to come through battle: the four of them against Mordred, his army, and his supernatural allies.

And so Spirit ended each day in the same way: by talking to Merlin.

Part of her remembered him as her old friend and counselor. The part that was Spirit did not know him as well, but trusted him as much as her other self did. And each night she went and spoke with him—sometimes alone, sometimes with the others—to try to find some weakness in Mordred's plans they could exploit.

TELL ME AGAIN WHAT HAPPENED THE NIGHT MORDRED ESCAPED FROM THE TREE, Spirit said. At first it had seemed very strange to receive her mentor's wise counsel through glowing letters on a sheet of glass, but the longer Spirit possessed her Reincarnate memories, the more her other self seemed to learn. At least the things she did over and over stopped seeming so jarringly strange.

THE NIGHT THE HELLRIDERS FOUGHT ONE ANOTHER AT THE PLACE THAT BECAME YOUR SCHOOL, FRIEND SLEW FRIEND, THROUGH MORDRED'S INFLUENCE, FOR THE PLACE OF THE GALLOWS OAK WAS EVER A FELL RESORT. THE DEATH BLOOD OF THE INNOCENT VICTIM WAS ENOUGH TO WEAKEN THE SPELLBOND THAT HELD HIM CAPTIVE.

BUT ONLY HIS SPIRIT GOT OUT, Spirit said. HIS BODY'S STILL IN THE OAK, AND HIS SPIRIT HAS POSSESSED KENNY HAWKING. DO YOU THINK HE'S STILL ALIVE?

There was a pause as Merlin thought. I FEAR KENNETH HAWKING'S SPIRIT IS GONE FOREVER, he said. BUT HIS DEATH PROVIDES OUR ONLY HOPE. IN SENDING HIS SPIRIT FORTH TO TENNANT HAWKING'S BODY, MORDRED HAS MADE HIMSELF VULNERABLE. . . .

I DON'T SEE HOW, Spirit answered crossly. IT MAKES HIM MORE INVULNERABLE, NOT LESS. IF WE KILL HIS "DOCTOR AMBROSIUS" BODY, ALL HE HAS TO DO IS RETREAT INTO THE TREE AGAIN.

"Hey." Burke walked into the control room and leaned

over the back of her chair. He glanced over the lines of chat. She looked up and smiled at him, even though it was difficult these days for Spirit to separate her awareness of him as Arthur from her awareness of him as Burke. She wasn't sure which of the two she loved—but then, most of the time Spirit wasn't really sure who *she* was, either.

"What happens if we kill Mordred's real body first? Burn the Oak?" he asked.

"You know as well as I do that the Kinslayer cannot die," Spirit answered crossly. "No weapon can slay him."

"It's been a long time since Merlin sealed him up in the Tree, though," Burke said doggedly.

"Okay then!" Spirit snapped. MERLIN. BURKE WANTS TO KNOW WHAT WOULD HAPPEN IF WE DESTROYED THE TREE BEFORE WE KILLED MORDRED?

Assuming we could actually fight our way through the Legions of Hell and do that, she added mentally.

There was so long a pause that Spirit began to wonder if they'd lost the connection, but the screen was still lit and the cursor was still blinking. At last, letters appeared on the screen.

IF HIS STOLEN BODY WERE KILLED, IT IS AS YOU HAVE SAID: MORDRED'S SPIRIT WOULD RETREAT INTO HIS TRUE BODY. BUT IT IS HIS MALIGNANT SPIRIT WHICH RENDERS HIS TRUE BODY UNKILL-ABLE. SEPARATED AS THEY ARE, HIS TRUE BODY CAN BE DESTROYED. AND WITHOUT HIS TRUE BODY TO SERVE AS REFUGE, MORDRED CAN BE KILLED IN HIS STOLEN FLESH.

"Then by fortune and by the grace of the Light, we may end the peril of the black serpent, Mordred Kinslayer, forever," Burke said. Like all of them, his speech swerved between High Forsoothly and normal, but Spirit was getting used to it. It was as if she'd lived a life as Guinevere, and then lived a second one as Spirit. Of the hundreds of lives she—Guinevere—must have lived between those two, she had no memory. It was the same for the other three, she knew.

"Reach Oakhurst, destroy the Tree, and there won't be anything left of Mordred. Then slay his stolen body to finish the job. Without him, the Shadow Knights will probably give up the idea of turning Earth into a radioactive cinder," Spirit said.

Defeat Mordred, and there would be an end to the eternal rebirth.

She wondered if it would feel like dying.

"And even if they don't, they'll be leaderless," Burke answered. "Ask Merlin if it'll work."

IF WE DESTROY THE GALLOWS OAK, AND THEN KILL MORDRED, WILL HE BE TRULY DESTROYED? Spirit typed. HIM, HIS MAGIC, EVERYTHING?

NOT ONLY HIS FELL AND STOLEN FLESH, BUT ALL HIS MAGIC, Merlin answered. ALL HE HAS SUMMONED AND CONJURED WILL PASS AWAY. YET THIS IS A PATH FILLED WITH DIFFICULTY AND PERIL, MY QUEEN.

Spirit always felt a little strange when Merlin addressed her by Guinevere's royal title. It was as if Merlin thought of Spirit White as a convenient and temporary fiction, and Guinevere of Britain as her true self. And Spirit only wished things were that clear cut.

THEN THAT'S WHAT WE'LL DO, she answered. GO TO OAKHURST, DESTROY THE TREE, AND THEN DESTROY MORDRED.

Somehow.

THEN I GIVE YOU GOODNIGHT, MY LADY, Merlin responded. AND WISH YOU SWEET REST TO PREPARE YOU FOR BATTLE.

GOODNIGHT, MERLIN, Spirit answered, and began the elaborate process of shutting the machinery of the computer control console down.

"I'd feel a little better about things if he wished us luck," Burke said.

"Merlin's a magician," Spirit answered absently. "He doesn't believe in luck." She sighed deeply. "I don't think this is going to be as easy as I made it sound," she added.

Burke chuckled. "Nothing ever is."

*

It was just before sunrise in the first week of April, and Spring had finally come for real. The dawn woods were mist-shrouded when Addie let the black van ghost to a stop and the four of them climbed out. She'd taken a roundabout route, driving cross country, to hide the van in the trees. It would be a several mile walk to reach Oakhurst, but Spirit had wanted to see how matters stood in Radial, particularly the state of The Fortress. *It probably won't be that easy, but it would be nice to think it could be,* Spirit thought.

They were all dressed identically in low sturdy boots, and pants and tunics in mottled woodland camouflage, and hooded cowls to cover their hair. The Cauldron Hallow was where their clothes had come from—an uneasy compromise between the modern day and their Reincarnate memories. In had gone the secondhand sweats, out had come these outfits.

"Follow me," Loch whispered. He moved noiselessly through the trees, slowly enough for the others to follow. But as they reached the edge of the trees. . . .

"Uh." Loch sounded disturbed. "This is bad."

Spirit hurried forward to stand beside him. She saw what he'd seen. "Yes it is," she said flatly.

The town was gone as if it had never been. The roads, the outlying houses—gone. The lake Addie had created during their escape from the Spring Fling was still here, currently covered in morning mist. A mile or so to the east of it stood The Fortress. Of all the buildings in what had once been Radial, only it was unchanged. Surrounding it now stood a Bronze Age village of huts. The people were already going about their daily tasks. It was somehow more horrible that they weren't dressed in RenFaire outfits, but in the dirty and torn twenty-first-century work clothes of their former lives.

"Ohhhh. . . ." Spirit said softly, looking at them. "I can—"

"What?" Burke asked.

"I can see what he did to them," Spirit said, amazed. "No

wonder Mordred didn't want to teach the School of Spirit. It's where his Gift comes from."

"A magician can never be fooled by a spell from their own School," Burke said in satisfaction.

"So that's why Mordred was so insistent on having the Macalister kids at the Spring Fling," Loch said. "He must have used them to get at their families."

"Contagion," Spirit said bleakly. "He'd have to be close by to ensorcell them. It would be so convenient to let them spread the spell themselves. Anyone without a Gift would be affected, so anyone who showed up to investigate would fall under it too."

"It's probably how he's planning to control the refugees after he launches the missiles," Burke said.

"But why would he—?" Addie asked, staring out at the newly-medieval village of Radial.

"Serfs," Loch said. "He needs laborers. To— To till the soil, bring in the crops, do all the scutwork. Sure, he's a magician— but I can't see him wasting his time using his power to bring in the harvest."

"He's re-creating what he knows," Spirit said, reasoning it out. "You— I— All of us, all of the Reincarnates, we *remember* that time, yes. But we also remember being born as who we are now."

"And the Kinslayer doesn't," Loch said in a hard voice.

"No," Spirit said. "And that's just one more reason we have to make sure he doesn't get the chance to remake the world."

"If we're going to lift this spell, we need allies," Loch said. "Come on."

✦

The village was a work in progress. Spirit wasn't sure where the houses and buildings that had been here before had gone—not even their basements remained—and the new village was clustered around the walls of The Fortress, just as a village would have been clustered around the walls of the castle in medieval times. She could see the places where the foundations of new huts had been laid out, and near the lake there was a place where mud bricks were being made. The huts they passed were one-room cottages. Some of the doors were open, and they could see makeshift beds inside. The huts were already empty—by this time in the morning, good little medieval villagers were already in the fields. The people Spirit and the others could see were working with hoes and rakes— not even a horse-drawn plow.

At the outer edge of the village was a hut twice the size of the others. Brenda Copeland was standing in the open doorway, tossing handfuls of grain to the ducks and chickens in the yard. Spirit glanced at her friends, unsure of what to do now, but before she could make up her mind, Brenda caught sight of the four of them.

"My lady—my lords," she gasped, dropping to her knees. Grain spilled everywhere, and the ducks and chickens swarmed her, trying to get the food.

Spirit heard Addie stifle a despairing giggle. How could something be funny and horrible at the same time?

"Get up," Spirit said desperately. "I— You have to come with me right now."

Brenda looked puzzled, but didn't argue. There was a stand of trees across the field behind The Fortress. As soon as they got there, Spirit relaxed a little. At least now they couldn't be seen as easily.

"How may I serve you?" Brenda said humbly.

"Tell me what you remember," Spirit said.

"I don't understand." Brenda stared at her in bafflement.

"Your name is Brenda Copeland," Spirit said carefully. "You live in the town of Radial, Montana. Your father is the Sheriff. And . . . something happened to you on March 22nd. Do you remember the Spring Fling?"

Suddenly Brenda's face filled with horrified awareness. She opened her mouth to scream, but Burke lunged forward and clapped his hand over her mouth.

"We're here to help!" Spirit said as Brenda struggled. "If you draw their attention, they'll kill us all!"

"Do you understand?" Loch asked. Brenda nodded, and Burke slowly took his hand away from her mouth.

"I . . . What's going on?" Brenda demanded, her voice shaky. "I went to the dance at Oakhurst. I remember thinking the decorations were creepy, and then— And then. . . ." Her voice trailed off, and there was a long moment of silence. "You said you'd tell me what was going on," she said at last. "After the Library. You said you'd tell me what was going on, and you never did."

Spirit took a deep breath. This was a good sign—she'd promised Brenda an explanation after the Shadow Knights had attacked the Town Library, but she'd never had the chance to deliver it. "This is going to sound freaky," she warned, then launched into the explanation: Oakhurst was a school for orphaned magicians. Dr. Ambrosius was the one who made them orphans. Dr. Ambrosius was actually an incredibly ancient evil necromancer who intended to take over the world and become its evil overlord.

"So you're all . . . witches?" Brenda asked, when Spirit was done.

"Magicians," Addie corrected automatically. "That's what they called us up at Oakhurst anyway."

Brenda looked around, her eyes still wild, and then down at herself. She was barefoot, her feet filthy, wearing muddy blue jeans, a T-shirt far too large for her, and a tattered barn coat. Spirit could see her mouth quiver as she fought back tears. No matter what Spirit had gone through in the last couple of weeks, at least she'd had some idea of what to expect. Brenda's world had been turned inside-out and upside-down in an instant.

"I— Can you— Can you fix my dad?" Brenda asked. "He's the Sheriff. He can help."

Maybe he can, Spirit thought, but before she could answer, Burke spoke up.

"I don't think that's a good idea, Brenda." The soft hesitancy Spirit was used to hearing in Burke's voice was gone now. It was hard to think of him as he'd been when she first met him. Now when she looked at him she saw Arthur, High King of Britain, not Burke Hallows, high school student.

"Your father is a good man," Burke said. "Never doubt that. But if he tries to be the Sheriff here and now, Breakthrough will kill him. And I don't even want to try to explain to him about the fact that magic is real—at least you'd had a taste of it before today. He hasn't. For now, he's safer where he is."

"But. . . . If you aren't going to break this, this *spell* over everyone, what *are* you going to do?" Brenda asked, a little desperately.

This time Burke waited for Spirit to speak. "We're going to Oakhurst, to free any of the other students being held prisoner there," Spirit said.

"You'll need some help," Brenda said. "Come on."

Addie glanced at Spirit. Spirit shrugged. She didn't think Brenda intended to betray them after what she'd seen.

Brenda led them through the maze of the village until they reached a small hut on the far edge. The door was open, and Veronica Davenport stood inside working at a long table. It was covered in mounds of green plants.

"Oh my god," Veronica said when she saw them. "What are you doing here? I thought you were dead!"

"Wait," Loch said. "You know who we are?"

Veronica frowned. "Of course I do. Oh god, I hope this

isn't some kind of a trap. I've been playing along since the Dance. . . ."

"It isn't," Spirit said quickly. "But what do you mean, you've been 'playing along'?"

Veronica beckoned them inside and pulled the door shut. The hut was stuffy and dark, but at least it got them out of sight.

"You guys ran off from the Dance," she said. "Nobody knew what was going on. Your friend in the black dress . . . she looked really sick. Is she . . . ?"

"She's dead," Addie said harshly. Veronica winced.

"I'm sorry," she said quietly. "I. . . . After the last Dance Committee meeting, when you were all so scared, we thought there had to be something weird about Oakhurst. But it didn't seem. . . . Well, everyone thought we'd better go anyway." She shrugged.

"So what happened after we left?" Burke asked.

"About half an hour later, the Headmaster guy, Ambrosius, came and said everything was fine, but it would be better if everyone went home. He sent all the Oakhurst kids back to their rooms, and when they were gone he said he was sorry our evening had been spoiled, but he had presents for us to make up for it. They wheeled in this big cart with a bunch of little bags on it—you know, like wedding favors or something? And everybody had to take one. Then we all left. A lot of guys just tossed theirs out the car windows on the way back to town. I threw mine out as soon as I got home. I had nightmares that night, and when I woke up . . . everything was

gone. My house. The town. And everybody was acting crazy."
She looked at Brenda. "I went to you. I tried to talk to you. But
it was like you'd turned into somebody else. I got scared."
She looked back at Burke and continued her story. "A few
people were still normal. It was horrible. They, you know, they
tried to wake up the others, or leave. But anybody who didn't
play along got stomped. I saw them—the Breakthrough guys,
all dressed up like knights or something—round up everyone who was fighting back. They had these, I don't know,
clubs or truncheons or something. If you resisted, you got
hit. . . ."

"Do you think anyone else escaped?" Loch asked.

Veronica shook her head. Her eyes filled with tears. "A few
of the people they took away came back, and then they were
happy little RenFaire zombies. Most of them . . . didn't."

"It's like some kind of a weird play, and everybody got assigned parts," Loch said blankly.

"Yes!" Veronica agreed eagerly. "That's exactly it. And
no matter what we saw, everyone else acted like it was all
normal. . . ."

She glanced toward Brenda, and Brenda shuddered. "I didn't
used to believe in monsters," she said softly.

"Yeah, well, welcome to our world," Loch said.

"Why didn't it affect me? What is it? What's going on?"
Veronica demanded.

Burke gave her a version of the same speech Spirit had
given to Brenda. "It's mind-control magic, I guess," he finished.
"At Oakhurst, we're taught that some people are harder to

affect than others. If you hadn't played along, they'd just have hit you with a bigger whammy."

Or you would have just vanished, Spirit thought.

"Lucky me," Veronica said bitterly. "But what do we do now?"

"We've got to rescue the others," Brenda said strongly. "Maybe some of them are just playing along—or maybe you can wake them up like you did me."

Spirit looked at Burke. The more time they spent here, the more dangerous it would be. On the other hand, she really wanted to test whatever power she had before she went to Oakhurst. What if everyone there had been overshadowed somehow?

"You can't just leave everyone here!" Brenda said desperately, when nobody said anything.

"No," Spirit said. "Of course we can't. And we're going to fix what Mordred did to them. But right now we need to get up to the school. We need to find out what's going on there."

"And save your friends first," Brenda said bitterly.

"Haven't you been paying attention?" Loch demanded. "Nobody has friends at Oakhurst if they're smart."

There was an awkward silence, since it was obvious the four of them were friends. And what did that make them?

Maybe not that smart, Spirit admitted.

"We really need to get out of here," Addie said.

"Brett and Juliette," Brenda said insistently. "We have to try to save them. You owe it to them. They were at the Library. And they're the only other ones left from the Committee."

Burke sighed faintly.

"Okay," Spirit said. "But we aren't going to go walking around this place. Can you bring them here?"

"I know where they are," Veronica said. "Wait here." She opened the door to the hut and looked nervously around, then hurried out.

"What if. . . . What if she's going to tell the overseers?" Brenda said nervously, voicing the same thought all of them had. "She said the thing, the spell thing, didn't affect her, but what if . . . ?"

"We're trusting all of you," Spirit said firmly. "We have to." *But what if she's right?*

It was a long, tense wait before Veronica returned. They could hear Brett and Juliette arguing with her; the two of them were worried about not completing their assigned tasks in time.

The door of the hut opened.

Brett and Juliette had been the king and the queen of Macalister High. Two weeks spent as medieval serfs had changed both of them far more than even Mordred could have imagined. Juliette's nails were chipped and broken and her long blonde hair was lank and greasy. Brett had a bruise on one cheekbone. Both of them had lost weight. They stopped dead at the sight of Spirit and the others, their eyes wild with fear. Then they dropped into clumsy obeisances.

Whatever Mordred did to everyone, he must have given them the ability to sense magic, Spirit realized. *That's why everyone under his spell thinks we're lords and ladies.* Even thought Spirit knew she wasn't one, it was hard to remember with Guinevere's memories so strong in her mind.

"You're Brett and Juliette Weber," Spirit said firmly. "This is the town of Radial. You're students at Macalister High School. Members of the Dance Committee. Two weeks ago you went to the Spring Fling at Oakhurst. *Remember!*"

The two of them stared up at Spirit for a long moment. Then Brett's expression changed. He lunged to his feet. "I'm getting out of here!" he cried.

Burke grabbed him before he could reach the door. Juliette was on her feet as well. She stared at Spirit with hate in her eyes.

"*You* did this to us!" Juliette said. "You and that bunch of freaks up at Hogwarts! This is all your fault!"

Two weeks ago Spirit would have been stunned and unable to respond, but not now. "It is not our fault," she said firmly. *I guess having been High Queen of England is good for something.* "We, too, are the victims of our true enemy. Ask your friends if you won't believe me. But heedless flight will only bring your doom."

"Good going," Addie murmured softly. The sarcasm in her voice was plain: the more Spirit sounded like a refugee from a road show company of *Camelot*, the less believable anything she said was.

Brett stopped struggling, and Burke released him.

"It's true," Veronica said. "They're in as much trouble as we are. More—they're from Oakhurst."

"Well maybe— Maybe we can *trade* them," Brett said desperately.

"For what?" Loch asked in disgust. "You think Mordred's going to just let you go?"

"We have a safe place to take you," Spirit said quickly. "We'll get you out of here and come back for your friends."

It took longer than it had with Veronica or Brenda to quiet the Webers down. They finally calmed down enough to confirm what Brenda had said—they didn't remember anything after the Dance. They'd thrown away the gift bags even before they reached their car that night. It didn't seem to make much difference.

"We hear—or I've heard, anyway—cars coming by the town," Veronica said. "But only at night. During the day, we only see horses."

"Those are the overseers," Brett said in a low dangerous voice. "From the castle."

Burke gave Spirit a worried look. He knew as well as she did that the Webers were trouble. Veronica had gotten time to adjust to this bizarre world, and Brenda was a natural problem-solver. Brett and Juliette were terrified and clearly on the edge of panic.

There was no help for it now. She couldn't re-cast Mordred's spell over them even if she'd been willing to.

"Come on," she said.

"And keep your mouths shut," Loch added.

FÍVE

The four Reincarnates and the four liberated Townies
headed back into the woods at the edge of the field. Spirit
and her friends kept the Radial teens in the middle of the
party. Once the eight of them were undercover, Loch started
to lead them in the direction of Oakhurst. Spirit put a hand on
his arm and shook her head, pointing toward the van. She
didn't want to take the Townies into Oakhurst. At least the
four of them had their magic—and months of commando
training, courtesy of their teachers. All the Radial kids had,
just now, was fear. And that could easily be turned against them
by Mordred and his allies.

Loch didn't look happy about Spirit's decision, but he nodded and began to lead all of them deeper into the trees.

"I don't understand why this is happening," Brenda said

plaintively. "Even if you *are* a wizard, you can't just make a whole town vanish. Somebody will notice."

"Sure," Burke said unconvincingly.

"You know what's going on," Juliette said accusingly. "I know you do. You have to tell us! You *owe* us!"

"When we're safe," Spirit said, gritting her teeth. It was bad enough having to tell them the villain of the piece was calling himself Mordred without explaining they were all the reincarnations of Arthurian myths and Mordred was going to bomb Earth back into the Stone Age.

When they were near the van, Loch stopped. He glanced back at Spirit, his face questioning.

"We drove here in a van. It's over there," Spirit said, pointing, keeping her voice low. "Go there and wait for us. We'll be back as soon as we can."

Brett looked as if he wanted to argue, but Veronica put a hand on his arm. "Come on," she said. "At least you won't be out in the field, right?"

Brett nodded reluctantly.

"You— You're coming back, right?" Brenda asked nervously.

"Of course we are," Addie said instantly. "We won't leave you. But you'll be safer here than if we take you with us." Before the others could say anything further, she turned and walked away.

❋

"Wow," Burke said comprehensively, as soon as they were sure they were out of earshot.

"I think they're doing pretty good, all things considered," Loch said. "At least there hasn't been any screaming."

"Yet," Addie said darkly. "They're going to be asking all the same questions we were asking two weeks ago—like why don't we just go to the cops?"

"Maybe we can," Spirit said. "If we can destroy the Tree, Mordred may panic."

"Aye," Burke said heavily. "The Kinslayer was always a coward."

*

They circled wide around the school grounds, sticking to cover as much as possible. It was mid-morning by the time they reached the stables, the buildings farthest away from the school itself.

"Is anyone still here?" Addie asked in bewilderment. There was no one anywhere in sight.

"The horses are," Loch said, coming back from a cautious inspection. "I guess that makes sense, if they're using them to patrol. But I don't see any people."

"Well, if there's nobody still here, it'll be a lot easier to break in," Burke said. "But they wouldn't just abandon Oakhurst. They'd take everything they could move down to The Fortress. And we haven't seen any sign of that. Let's keep looking."

"Carefully," Spirit said, and Burke smiled at her.

There'd been a lot of new construction on the campus since Breakthrough had moved in back in January. It made sneaking around a lot easier than it would have been other-wise. The new Security building was next to the Motor Pool, and the four of them could hear the sound of a walkie-talkie long before they saw the security guard in Breakthrough black. He looked bored.

Eavesdropping on the chatter over his radio, they could understand why. Most of the security staff seemed to be inside the school building. The students were confined to their rooms. The whole place was on lockdown.

"That's what we needed to know," Spirit said, her voice a mere whisper. Burke nodded. He crept around the side of the SUV and sprang at the bored guard.

"All clear," he said a moment later. "And I've got his keys."

⁂

They went in through the back way, the doors that over-looked the gardens and the path to the little train station, the doors she'd gone in and out of a dozen times a day when Oakhurst had still been nothing more to her than the school to which she'd been exiled by her family's death. The doors leading from the Refectory into the main part of the school stood open, but everything was changed. *It feels like sneaking into a haunted house,* Spirit thought. All the tables and chairs were stacked in the corners, and the room was filled with boxes. As Burke had said, they were clearly planning to gut Oakhurst to enrich The Fortress, but they hadn't quite fin-ished yet.

"We have to get to the Main Hall," Spirit said, keeping her voice low. That was where the Gallows Oak—and Mordred's entombed body—was.

"I'll scout ahead," Loch said.

Even with Spirit looking right at him, Loch just seemed to vanish. That was what the Shadewalking Gift did. It wasn't invisibility: it was more like misdirection refined into high art.

Loch was back less than five minutes later, seeming to simply appear out of thin air. It was as if he'd been there all along and she just suddenly noticed him. He didn't look happy.

"It looks like the Shadow Knights are having a party in the Main Hall," he said grimly. "There's no way we can walk in there and nuke the Tree."

"Now what?" Addie demanded despairingly.

"We need—" Spirit began.

"Company," Loch said in warning.

He indicated one of the storerooms off the kitchen, and they hurried to hide. It was completely empty. There wouldn't be a lot of reason for anyone to come in here. They held their collective breaths and strained to listen. In a moment, they heard voices coming from outside.

"I don't like this idea." The voice belonged to Mark Rider—Mark of Cornwall, Mordred's sworn knight. Spirit clutched Burke's arm, whipsawed between Spirit's terror and Guinevere's rage. Mark had been Arthur's sworn vassal before Mark betrayed him to ally himself with Mordred. . . .

"When I swore to him it was for wealth and power," Mark went on. "I make no secret of that. I never have. How much of either is there in a radioactive wasteland? I have no interest in ruling a kingdom of ashes."

"You should have considered that a long time ago, husband." Madison Lane-Rider's voice had the faintly formal inflection of her Reincarnate self, Morgause of Orkney. "Now your decisions all come down to one. Do you wish to live or die? Cross the Black Dragon, and you choose death."

Mark's only answer was a wordless growl, and the two of them passed on down the hall. It was a long time before Spirit could draw a deep breath.

"So much for convincing Mark to change sides," Addie muttered.

"As if," Loch whispered back, and Addie shrugged philosophically.

"Now what?" Burke asked Spirit.

"With the Shadow Knights in the Main Hall, we need two things: a way to destroy the Tree *fast,* and a big enough distraction to lure the Shadow Knights away while we do it. That means—" she swallowed hard, thinking of Doc Mac. "—that means we can't just do it ourselves. We need to find someone who has a Gift that can destroy the Tree—and who's willing to help us."

"If everybody's on lockdown, they'll probably be glad to do anything if it means getting out," Loch said. "By your leave—"

"No," Spirit said instantly, already knowing what he was

about to say. "We stay together. I'm the only one who can break a glamourie if— If any of you get, you know, *hit*."

"Lucky you; at least that's one less thing for us to worry about," Loch said without heat. "Come on, then. I'll take point. Where do you want to start?"

"Let's start with people who might actually be on our side," Spirit said.

"Dylan," Addie and Loch said in chorus.

Dylan Williams was the only other person who knew any of the secret truths of Oakhurst. He'd helped them spy on Mordred, and he'd listened to the recording that had proven that Dr. Ambrosius was their enemy. But he'd never been a member of their inner circle. Spirit could only hope he was willing to help them now.

And that they could trust him.

Dylan's room was on the second floor of the Young Gentleman's Wing. Sneaking around Oakhurst was creepy beyond imagining. Once upon a time they'd imagined a Shadow Oakhurst where kids without magic might be sent. Now Oakhurst itself had become a thing of shadows. With Loch to guide them—without him, they would have been completely lost several times over, with all the detours they had to make—they finally reached the Young Gentlemen's Wing. The hallway was entirely empty.

And more than empty.

"Where are the *doors?*" Addie asked in a strained voice.

Spirit had only been here once or twice, but she knew the layout of the Young Gentlemen's Wing was exactly like that of the Young Ladies' Wing: a hallway full of numbered doors that led to dorm rooms, as bland and forgettable as a corridor in an expensive hotel.

Not any more. Now, the entire hall was featureless, blank-walled, empty. The only door was the one that led to the second floor; aside from that, there wasn't a single door to be seen. Spirit tried to remember if she'd seen windows on the outside when they'd passed by the dorm wing, and couldn't.

"Transmutation could take care of that," Burke said. "Turn the doors into something soft, have someone smooth them flat, turn them back again into whatever. Easy."

"Just hope there wasn't anyone inside when they did that," Addie said, and all of them shivered.

"Come on," Loch whispered. He stepped into the hallway, and they followed.

The door to the second floor was locked, and none of the keys on the key ring Burke had taken from the security guard opened it. Spirit was about to suggest trying another door—or seeing if they could get in through the servants' wing—when Addie produced her Hallow. The first key she tried opened the lock, and she smiled effortlully.

"Useful," she said.

Spirit fingered the pen (the Sword) on its ribbon around her neck. They'd all brought their Hallows, but she wasn't sure she could bring herself to use hers. There weren't many things you could do with a sword besides hurt somebody.

Or kill them.

They all felt safer once they were in the stairwell. None of them could sense any spells in use—if there were kids being held prisoner here in this wing of the school, it was clear that Mordred was counting on nothing more mystical than locked doors to keep them where they were.

And why shouldn't he? Why wouldn't he expect them to just stay where they're told to? Spirit asked herself. *Most of the kids here have been at Oakhurst a lot longer than I was. And what's the one lesson everybody did their best to din into all of us? Unthinking obedience.*

They reached the second floor. Spirit took a deep breath of relief. The corridor looked normal: lined with doors on each side.

Loch walked halfway down the hall and turned toward a door on the left. "This is it," he said, gesturing at the door.

Addie brought out her keys again and unlocked it, then pushed it open. The room inside was dim. She was about to step inside, when Burke put a hand on her shoulder and eased her back from the door. He stepped through first, and a moment later Spirit saw why.

Dylan had been alerted by the sound of the key in the lock. He was hidden beside the door, the curtain rod in his hand. He swung at Burke before he realized who it was, but Burke caught the weapon easily.

"Hold on there," he said mildly.

"Oh my god, you came back?" Dylan said in disbelief and horror. "Get in here—*quick!*"

He dragged Burke inside, and the others followed. Spirit quietly shut the door behind her. She realized the room wasn't just dim, but as dark as if it was the middle of the night, and after a moment, she realized why.

It wasn't because the curtains were drawn.

It was because the glass of the windows had been turned to stone.

"Oh my god," Dylan repeated, sounding half hysterical. "Everyone was sure you guys were dead!"

"Muirin is," Loch said in a flat voice, and Dylan sucked in a long shaky breath.

"I'm sorry," he said honestly. "I. . . . I liked her a lot." He scrubbed his hands over his face. "What do you need?"

"Information," Spirit said instantly, concealing her surprise at the question. Dylan had hit the ground running. *He's a credit to Oakhurst,* she thought sardonically.

"Okay," Dylan said. "I don't know much. You guys bailed on the Spring Fling thing. We all got sent to our rooms pretty quick after that. Doc A—I guess we should all call him Mordred now, like you said—called a general assembly in the chapel the next day—not even in the Refectory or over e-mail—and said Radial wasn't in bounds any more. He said he'd had to launder the Townies' memories for our protection—not that anybody really believed that, not that it mattered much. There wasn't any more testing after the dance, either, so I guess it was you guys he was looking for. Anyway, classes were pretty much cancelled, and we were all stuck in our rooms twenty-four seven except for when we got herded down to the Refectory for meals. That lasted a couple of days, then they started delivering food to the dorms once a day—all the MREs you can eat—and we all got put on permanent lockdown. How it works is, they dump the food in the hall under guard, and then unlock our doors so we can go out and grab something. If you don't hustle, you don't get, either, because some of the guys are hoarding. About a third of us—not me—have been made into Proctors. They stay somewhere else, I think. Every two or three days we get herded out to the chapel again—just us, I guess the girls go on a different schedule—to hear a lecture about how our only hope for survival is to serve. I think they do it so we'll try to run for it. A couple of guys did." Dylan shuddered. "I never saw them again. Breakthrough has dogs now—Warded, so it doesn't matter if you have one of the Air Gifts." He gestured at his computer. "They took down the Intraweb, too. So much for doing a Spartacus and organizing a student uprising. . . ."

Spirit had only been half listening. She'd been more focused on looking. Dylan seemed to have a strange aura of magic around him. Nobody'd ever talked about being able to see magic in any of her classes. But she thought she knew what this was.

"*Wake up!*" she ordered, interrupting Dylan's ramblings.

He blinked, staring at her, and suddenly in his expression she could see the memories—the Reincarnate memories—flooding into his mind. And as they did, she knew him. So did the others.

"Well met, Gareth Beaumains," Loch said warmly, stepping forward and clasping Dylan's forearm in greeting. "Are you ready for the fight?"

"I . . ." Dylan was plainly still stunned. "My lord. My lady. . . . Oh, *euw*, Madison's my *mom*. And Ovcharenko's my *brother*."

"It takes a little getting used to," Spirit said. *If I needed any more proof that being a Reincarnate doesn't mean you have to be the same person you were, this would be it.* Gareth Beaumains was remembered in Arthurian Myth as The Kitchen Knight. He was the youngest son of Lot and Morgause, and Gawain, Agravaine, and Gaheris were three of his brothers.

Mordred was the fourth.

"Wow," Addie said, staring at Spirit. "You— You're—"

"You really do have magic." Spirit didn't need magic to guess what Addie was thinking. Vivianne—The Lady of the Lake— had kept a court nearly as grand as Arthur's, and tendered her aid to Arthur and Guinevere out of courtesy, not fealty.

Spirit tried to force the double vision out of her thoughts. Mordred was the one doing his best to live in the past, and Spirit had no intention of joining him there. But apparently they had one thing in common. They both had the School of Spirit magic that would allow them to awaken the Reincarnates.

Only Mordred had centuries more experience at it. The magic her Guinevere-self remembered was nothing like what Spirit had seen at Oakhurst.

While she was struggling with her thoughts—and with her new awareness of what she could do—Loch and Burke filled Dylan in on what they'd learned in the fortnight since their escape.

"We need to rally the good guys," Dylan said when they were done. "And the first step to doing that is to take back the Intraweb. That will take out their electronic security, too. I can do that. You guys need to find someone who can zap the Tree."

"Yes," Addie drawled. "We managed to figure that out for ourselves."

Dylan just laughed. It was a free and joyful sound, unlike anything Spirit had ever heard from him before. "I'd Jaunt it for you, but it's too big for me to move. But this fight is mine, for should you fall into their hands, my friends, our cause is— I mean, we'll be toast. I can get to the computer lab without being seen, I think. I can get the system up from there."

There was a moment of silence, and Spirit realized that all of them—even Burke—were waiting for her to say whether or not they'd follow Dylan's plan.

She nodded in reluctant agreement. It might not be a great plan, but she didn't have a better one. "Take—" she began, but before she could say Dylan should take Loch with him, Dylan was out the door and running.

"Now what?" she asked, not caring whether it was a Queenly thing to say or not.

"Well, anyone who's locked up in here is probably going to be on our side," Burke said.

"And I have the key to every lock," Addie said. "Come on!"

The others followed her as she ran out into the hall. Addie unlocked the doors one by one, moving along as soon as each door was open. Loch, Burke, and Spirit followed her, opening the doors and giving quick explanations.

"Surprise!" Spirit heard Loch say. "You aren't being rescued, run for your life." He sounded unreasonably cheerful about it, too.

In moments the hallway was full of scared—and angry— kids.

Burke and Loch called out the Gifts of everybody they freed. It would take Fire or Transmutation to affect Mordred's Oak, and none of the boys had it. Both Troy Lang— Transmutation—and Andrew Tate—Fire Witchery—were among the missing. The most powerful Gift someone who was still here possessed was Chris Terry's, and he was a Weather Witch. Most of the boys on the dorm floor had Air Gifts—Animal Communication, Weather Control, Illusion, or Pathfinding.

"Go on, get out of here. Head for the trees in the woods behind The Fortress," Spirit said over and over. "We have a place to go where we'll all be safe."

Some of them might be Reincarnates like Dylan, but Spirit didn't want to know one way or the other right now. It was too complicated to be dealt with in the middle of a jailbreak. And what if their Reincarnate selves wanted to side with Mordred?

They couldn't keep the boys with them once they'd liberated them, and they didn't even try. Everyone just scattered— Spirit could only hope the boys would remember the rendezvous point they'd been given. She and her friends had somewhere else to be.

As soon as everyone was freed from their bedrooms-turned-prisons, Spirit and her friends headed for the Young Ladies' Wing. But to get there, they needed to cross the Great Hall—and the Great Hall had become a madhouse, because that was the direction most of the boys had gone. While the Breakthrough Security people were doing their best to contain the student riot, they weren't really a match for a bunch of scared young magicians who'd spent months learning unarmed combat. The windows were shattered, the floor had buckled, and there were people everywhere.

Spirit skidded to a halt, staring at the Tree. Of all the things here in the Great Hall, it was the only one that was unchanged.

"Come on!" Burke said, grabbing her.

Spirit heard a ripping noise, and saw water come spraying up through the cracks in the floor—Addie, or one of the other Water Witches, was adding to the chaos. And it didn't take magic powers to sense an oncoming storm. By now there was so much noise it was impossible to talk and hard to think. But the one thing Spirit knew for sure was that she still had to find someone whose Gift could destroy the Tree. And the Girls' Dorm was the only place left to look. There might be a Fire Witch among the students still in lockdown.

They have to know where we're going, Spirit thought. But they had no choice.

Ahead of her she saw a security guard grab for Loch. Loch barely slowed down, but the guard went reeling back, clutching his throat. By the time the four of them reached the other wing, the door to the second floor had already been smashed open. The ground floor corridor was sealed and featureless like the one on the boys' side, but Spirit could hear shouting from the floor above. She doubted anybody had been able to force the bedroom doors, but she knew someone who could.

"Addie—*go!*" Spirit shouted. Addie nodded, and ran up the stairs.

The floor beneath Spirit's feet shook. She turned back the way she'd come, and just . . . stared.

The Breakthrough minions who'd been summoned to make sure nobody else escaped weren't human. There were three of them, each twelve feet tall, and muscled like the Incredible Hulk. They were wearing kilts and—Spirit stifled a hysterical giggle—red T-shirts with the Breakthrough logo on them.

Where did they ever find T-shirts in the right size?

Then the first one lunged forward, only to be knocked back as Burke activated the Shield and thrust it forward. The giant roared in fury—it sounded like a lion, only louder, not human at all—and attacked again.

But now Loch had evoked the Spear. He wasn't using it as a weapon—at least, not as a stabbing weapon. It spun in his hands like a quarterstaff, and every time it struck one of his enemies, Spirit could hear a sound like an ax hitting wood.

"*Go!*" Burke shouted to her. Spirit ran up the stairs.

The hall was filled with the girls from the Young Ladies' Wing. Every door that Addie hadn't unlocked had been smashed open. Spirit grabbed Emily Davis as she headed for the stairs.

"No!" Spirit shouted. "That way's blocked!"

But Emily wouldn't listen. She was too scared. She tore loose from Spirit and ran down the stairs.

"Listen everyone!" Spirit cried at the top of her lungs. "We have to find another way out of here!"

A girl named Vanessa Cartwright stared at her with fearful wide green eyes. She was a year older than Spirit. Spirit couldn't remember what her Gift was. Fire? Water? Suddenly it seemed urgent to remember.

All of a sudden there was an ear-splitting squeal. Spirit hadn't thought Oakhurst had a PA system, but of course it must. There had to have been a way to talk to everyone before there'd been e-mail.

"—*If he'd handled things quietly, Spirit White and Lachlan Spears would be dead now."* It was Mordred's voice.

Dylan's got the recording we made! He's playing it back!

"*These things take time, my lord. I assure you—*"

"*You're too used to living a masquerade for the mortal cattle I will soon rule. Do you really think it needs to look like an accident?*"

Everyone had stopped for a moment, transfixed by the recording.

"They have us blocked in!" Spirit shouted again, and this time they heard her. "We need to find another way out!"

"Fire escape!" It was Kelly Langley. "This way!" the Proctor (probably a former Proctor now) said. "Come on, everyone!"

Kelly wasn't the only Proctor who'd been in lockdown. Angelina Swanson—*well, I sure didn't see that coming,* Spirit thought. *Of all people to end up in Mordred's bad books*—joined Kelly and began bullying everyone into some semblance of order. The fire door was at the far end of the hall—or it had been. The wall had been sealed shut, the same way the doors downstairs had been. And nobody here had Transmutation, or they would already have opened it.

"Let me!" Spirit shouted, pushing through the milling crowd. She wanted to go back downstairs, to help Burke and Loch—if they were still alive—but she couldn't leave everyone here trapped. "I need some room!" she said, and Kelly and some of the others pushed the rest of the kids back.

It's different when it's real, Spirit thought. She clutched the pen in her hand, and suddenly it wasn't a pen any longer. It was a sword. *The* Sword. *"The Sword confers victory on the wielder."* Vivian's voice echoed in her thoughts.

She struck at the wall as hard as she could. It took her several tries to hack a hole, but the Transmuted door wasn't as thick as the rest of the wall. As soon as there was a hole, everyone surged in to help. The fire stairs were steep and narrow, but they led directly to the outside. Students started hurrying down them.

"You overstep yourself, Mark of Cornwall."

"Truth serves you better than empty flattery, my prince."

Dylan's bootleg recording reached its end and started over from the beginning. Spirit grabbed Kelly and dragged her back to the stairwell.

"We need to burn the Tree!" she shouted in Kelly's ear.

"We'll never make it!" Kelly shouted back. But she followed Spirit.

Addie was already at the door of the staircase leading down to the First Floor. The moment she saw Spirit running toward her, Addie turned and dashed down the stairs.

One of the giants was down, and Loch and Burke were double-teaming a second one. The hallway was too narrow for the enormous creature to close with them, but there was a third giant who was doing its best to force Loch and Burke out of the narrow space into the larger one beyond.

"*Kelly!*" Addie shouted.

The walls began to buckle and splinter as Addie called the water up out of the pipes. It burst out of the wall in a stinging spray—and then Kelly used her Fire Gift to turn it into steam. The jet of steam caught the second giant full in the face. It screamed—the most human sound Spirit had heard any of them make—and crashed to the ground. At the same time, Loch and Burke took out the last one.

The steam stopped.

"Come on!" Spirit said. "We have to get to the Tree! I've got Kelly!"

Burke grabbed her before she could dash out into the hall. "You can't! It's too well guarded! They're making their last stand to defend it. We have to get out of here!"

For a long agonized moment Spirit pulled back against Burke's grip. They were *so close.* . . . Finally she nodded.

"Let's go," Loch said.

Later, when it was all over, Spirit would barely remember the next few minutes. It was what her other self would have called 'a fighting retreat' as the five of them—Spirit, Addie, Loch, Burke, and Kelly—fought their way back the way they'd come. If not for the Shield Burke wielded, they would have been shot dead half-a-dozen times. But Burke used the Shield to cover their retreat, and most of the Breakthrough people took one look at the sword Spirit was carrying and ran. She was just as glad. Guinevere's memories or not, Spirit wasn't sure she could bring herself to kill somebody.

The five of them burst out of the building at a run.

"The stables!" Addie gasped. "We need horses!"

Spirit looked toward the stables. By Dylan's count, there were about thirty kids—forty at most—who hadn't gone over to the Dark Side. The last time Spirit had counted them, there'd been about three dozen horses in the stables. Everybody who'd escaped from the school was down at the paddock saddling horses. Finally all those horrible Endurance Ride lessons were coming in useful. And today the Oakhurst students weren't fighting each other. In fact, most of the horses were carrying double.

"Come on—come on!" Dylan rode toward them. "Hurry! They'll be after us in a minute!"

"Addie! Go with Dylan! Show everyone where to go!" Spirit cried.

Addie nodded briefly. Dylan reached down to her, and Addie swung herself up behind him. Dylan galloped off after the riders who'd already fled. The other four ran on toward the stables.

"They'll just run us down," Loch said as he ran. "Breakthrough. They've still got cars and trucks."

"No," Burke said. "They'd have to take the trucks right through Radial. They won't risk them being seen."

Spirit only hoped Burke was right.

"Maybe I can give them something else to think about," Kelly said determinedly. "All our guys are out of there, right?"

"I hope so," Spirit said fervently. Most of the other kids— and the horses—were already gone, but Gareth and Noah were in the paddock with four horses—saddled but without riders. They were obviously waiting for them.

"Okay then," Kelly said. She stopped, and turned back to face the building. "I never liked this place anyway," she said.

For a long moment nothing happened. Then there was the sound of shattering glass, the roar of an inferno, and smoke began to belch out of the third floor windows.

Spirit hoped the Tree was going to go up in the flames, but she was afraid that was too much to hope for. She followed the others toward the paddock.

Noah swung up behind Gareth, and Spirit and Loch took the second horse. Burke rode alone. He led the last of the horses, and Kelly grabbed it and vaulted into the saddle as they rode past her. By now the upper stories of the building were burning brightly.

"Won't last long," Kelly said in disappointment. "Or do

much damage. Half of Breakthrough has Water Gifts. But it should slow them down a little."

Then there was no more time for talk. Only for escape. It was a hellride to match the worst of the Endurance Rides. The horses took the main drive at a wild gallop. Spirit heard bullets spang off Burke's Shield, but mostly she concentrated on not falling off the horse.

Lachlan Spears had always been one of the better riders of their little group, but now he rode as if he could sense every move his horse would make before it made it. *The most graceful man a-horse,* Spirit thought distractedly.

Ahead of them—in what used to be the outskirts of Radial—Spirit could see the rest of the horses and riders. Everyone was strung out in a long ragged line—the better animals and riders in the lead, the others straggling behind. Gareth had saved them some of the best horses available, so Spirit and the others with her quickly overtook the stragglers.

If the range of the Command and Control Gifts had been any larger, Oakhurst's fleeing refugees would have been in more trouble than they were right now, but by the time Mordred and his minions realized what they were doing, their horses were too far away for the Shadow Knights to affect.

The sky was black with the oncoming storm summoned either by Oakhurst students or Breakthrough mages. Spirit could see lightning striking in the distance, somewhere on the other side of what was left of Radial. She hoped some of it was hitting The Fortress. The horses, not galloping now so much as bolting uncontrollably, charged through the emptiness that had been a town two weeks ago, and then across fields full of bespelled townsfolk. The people scattered as the horses thundered past.

Is this too easy? Spirit wondered desperately. *Are they just setting a trap?*

She hoped with all her heart that it wasn't, that they weren't, that the element of surprise in their attack on Oakhurst had been enough to confuse Breakthrough, Mordred, and the Shadow Knights. Mordred knew he couldn't let them escape, but he might be counting on being able to track them on horseback, and Spirit knew there had to be more horses at The Fortress. Maybe he wasn't striking them down now because he figured he could find them the old-fashioned way.

Now Spirit could see riderless horses. Some were bolting in panic, others were galloping along beside the other horses. She didn't see anybody on foot or on the ground, so the riderless horses had to mean the first of the refugees had reached the van.

How are we going to fit everyone inside? Spirit thought in sudden horror. *There are dozens of us, and the van won't hold more than twenty at most. We can't leave anyone behind. . . .*

There were still a dozen riders behind her and Burke when Burke reined in at the foot of the hill. Burke leaped from the saddle and began running up the slope. Addie must already be at the van. Spirit staggered as her feet touched the ground. Loch grabbed her to steady her, and began dragging her up the hill. She pulled away to look back in the direction of the town as Kelly passed her. There were horses galloping out of the front gates of The Fortress. Their leader carried a banner with the Breakthrough logo on it, and dogs ran beside them. It was all like something out of an old movie—or a historical novel.

Or a nightmare.

She turned and followed Loch and Kelly up the hill.

"—stupid idiotic fool!"

The first thing she heard was Addie's voice raised in fury.

"Why should I think you were coming back?" That was Brett. Whining. The sound of his voice set Spirit's teeth on edge. "Besides, it didn't work."

Spirit reached the van. The driver side window was smashed out, and the hood was sprung. Clearly Brett Weber had tried to hotwire the black van. Just as clearly, it hadn't worked.

"And you think not managing to run out on us with our only transportation is a point in your favor?" Loch snapped. "I should—"

"Well, you were going to ditch some of us anyway, because this thing won't take all of us," Brett whined. "So I figure I didn't have anything to lose. Now we're all in the same boat," he finished in a gloating tone.

"Get out of my way!" Addie snapped. She shoved past Brett with more energy than the motion required. Spirit saw him stagger.

"Nobody's being left behind," Spirit said firmly. Brett's rash remark was having an effect; the Oakhurst students gathered behind her were looking worried. "Van," she said, picking someone at random. "Do you know who was in lockdown from the girls' side? Is everyone here?"

Her question had the desired effect. The Oakhurst kids had a good idea of who'd been recruited and who hadn't. "Everybody who was in lockdown from our wing is here," Vanessa answered. "I don't know about the boys."

Before Spirit could find someone to ask about the boys, Burke came back from the edge of the wood.

"Eight more on the way," he said. "That's everyone in sight."

Suddenly Spirit heard the engine of the van roar into life. Black smoke curled from under the sprung hood, and more broken glass jingled free of the shattered side window. Then suddenly its outline shimmered, and as Spirit watched, the van changed its shape, growing into the familiar form of a big yellow school bus.

"It isn't an illusion!" Addie called out the window. "It's real! Everybody get on board!"

Loch jumped aboard immediately, and that was all the Oakhurst kids needed to see in order to take this new weirdness in stride. They followed Loch aboard the bus immediately. The four kids from Radial stood and stared as the Oakhurst kids climbed aboard, then Brett moved into the line, and the others followed. Spirit hung back, making sure there wasn't any pushing or fights—she saw Brett get the idea of pushing to the front of the line, and abandon it after he got a good look at the muscles on the Oakhurst boys—and girls.

As soon as Spirit was sure he wouldn't change his mind—or make some other kind of trouble—she went to help Burke bring the last of the students up the hill. In the distance, she could see that the mounted Shadow Knights were getting a lot closer.

"Come on," she said, grabbing the nearest girl's arm.

It was Kylee, and as Spirit touched her, she felt the tingle of magic. Kylee was another Reincarnate: Spirit could awaken Kylee's Reincarnate self with a single word. *Do I have the right?* she thought distractedly. *This is a heck of a time to be worrying about that!*

Spirit and Burke were the last ones onto the bus. Every seat was filled, and some people were sitting in the aisle. Addie yanked the door shut and the bus started moving—slowly, ponderously—up the hill. There was a farm road at the top of the hill, Spirit remembered. Just a dirt track, but it joined the feeder road that led to the Interstate.

As soon as she reached the road Addie floored the accelerator. The bus slid, shimmied, and lurched. It had started raining while they were still under the trees, and the windshield wipers slapped heavily against the windshield while sprays of mud blurred the windows. Spirit clung to the back of the driver's seat and tried to use the rearview mirror to check for pursuit. She didn't see anything, but then, she couldn't see much at all. *Horses don't like to be out in heavy rain,* she told herself, something she knew from her Endurance Riding classes. Horses liked to be dry, and warm, and home in their nice comfy stalls when the weather was bad, and even if their riders didn't, dealing with cranky horses would slow them down.

"Can't this go any faster?" Juliette Weber demanded.

"It's a magic school bus, not a Sherman Tank," Addie answered tartly.

Suddenly the entire bus lurched violently as Addie made a sharp right turn. Several people screamed as they slid out of their seats and onto the floor. Spirit got a blurred glimpse through a mud-smeared window of an official-looking sign saying "Do Not Enter," and suddenly they were on the Interstate.

"Hang on!" Addie shouted, gunning the engine.

Spirit saw the flash of headlights coming straight toward them. *We're on the wrong side!* she thought in panic. Then Addie was across the divider and back onto the road, the bus fishtailing as she fought to get it going in the right direction.

"I guess there isn't anything I need to teach you about defensive driving," Loch said into the momentary silence.

SIX

It was several long hours on the road before they reached the missile silo once more. Long enough for Spirit to tell everyone the whole story about Oakhurst: that Doctor Ambrosius was really the evil sorcerer Mordred, that he'd orphaned everyone who had magic, that he intended to start a war so he could rule the world.

It sounded more ridiculous each time she said it, but nobody laughed. After spending the last two weeks locked in their rooms, the Oakhurst kids might not believe the whole story she was telling them, but they certainly believed something horrible was going on. Some of them had still been wearing their class rings when they'd fled the school, but Spirit had made sure everyone threw them away while they were still on the bus. And even the four kids from Radial, to whom all the talk about sorcery and wizard wars was new and unbelievable, didn't scoff. Having woken up to see their town turned into a medieval village seemingly overnight, the Townies knew better than to say anything was impossible.

After the round of obvious questions (why didn't they go to the police or the FBI or the government?) everybody settled down to a weary silence. Fortunately, Addie's Cauldron-magic was able to feed them along the way, and between Loch and Addie, they managed to find a much shorter route than the original one QUERCUS had given Spirit. But Spirit still had plenty of time to worry about the next thing. What were they going to do when they got to the silo? Maybe Addie could work her Cauldron-magic to keep all of them fed, but where were they all going to sleep? How was she going to convince everyone not to just go running off to find the nearest phone?

The only part Spirit had left out of her explanation had been the stuff about the Reincarnates. She was the only one who could awaken the memories of the Grail Knights (unless Addie, Burke, or Loch could do it too, but somehow she didn't think they could), and she still couldn't decide how she felt about that, especially after watching Dylan's reaction to being Awakened.

Dylan was sitting halfway to the back of the bus, pale and silent, just as he'd been ever since he'd rejoined them. She was more relieved by his silence than she wanted to admit to herself. She didn't want Dylan telling everyone he was really Gareth Beaumains, and they were all spear-carriers in an Arthurian Myth.

Although Loch's the only one with an actual spear. . . .

The reason Dylan was following her lead, Spirit suspected, was because he recognized her, Burke, and Loch. Gareth Beaumains had been a knight of the Round Table. That wouldn't work for everyone, because she knew from hearing about the Shadow Knight Reincarnates that not all of them had been from Arthur's Court—or even on Arthur's side. But despite the additional problems that came with adding three-dozen refugees—and possible Reincarnates—to the people she had to watch over, Spirit couldn't really regret having done it.

If she'd waited any longer, she wasn't sure there would have been anyone left to rescue.

When they finally reached the abandoned missile field, Spirit received her first *good* surprise of the day. There was a familiar figure standing beside the shack that led down into the control silo.

"Vivian!" she cried, as Addie brought the bus to a halt.

Spirit pushed her way out the doors before Addie got them completely open. She ran to Vivian and hugged her very hard. "You came back!"

"I . . . So I did, my lady," Vivian said awkwardly.

It didn't take much for Spirit to understand the source of her unease. She might be Vivian, but she was also the Reincarnate Nimue. Mordred's pawn, jailer of The Merlin. And now, she knew that Spirit—Guinevere—knew it.

"That was a long time ago," Spirit said, answering the unspoken words. "And you have more than redeemed yourself. But I'm so glad to see you—I thought you'd left forever!"

"I was lucky enough to return. And not alone." Vivian gestured behind her, where a familiar figure was coming out from behind the building.

"Elizabeth!" Spirit said in joyful disbelief. Of all the people who had vanished, Elizabeth was the one Spirit had figured was most certainly gone forever. "I thought you were dead!"

"I would have been," Elizabeth Walker said, smiling wearily. "But the Shadow Knights wanted information I did not have, and were careful to preserve me in hopes of gaining it. They thought I must know where The Merlin hid, because I had regained my Reincarnate memories."

Spirit glanced around quickly. Everyone was getting off the bus now, looking around and asking Addie, Loch, and Burke where they were and what was going on. "I've told them almost everything," she said quickly. "But I haven't told them that part."

"But you must!" Elizabeth said instantly. "Even *I* can see that many of them are Reincarnates, though I know not of whom, for the magic lies heavy upon them. They deserve to know."

"They deserve a little peace," Spirit said, more sharply than she meant to. "What use is a headful of ancient history?"

Elizabeth might have said something more, but everyone was coming off the bus now, and Vivian had moved to greet them.

"Hi, everyone. My name is Vivian." Vivian, to Spirit's relief, was taking immediate charge of the mob of rescuees, just as she had of the four of them not so long ago. "And believe it or not, I'm an actual Oakhurst alumni. It's great to see you all, and fortunately I knew you were coming."

How? Spirit mouthed at Elizabeth.

Scrying Gift, Elizabeth mouthed back. Vivian was a Water Witch, but Elizabeth—Iseult—had the Gift of Prophecy. Scrying.

"The accommodations aren't great, but they're better than Oakhurst—well, I mean the concentration camp that Oakhurst turned into," Vivian went on. "Come on and we'll get everyone settled. After that, I'll take questions."

Oh, good one, Vivian. Remind them what they escaped. That's smart, Spirit thought admiringly.

"Hey, uh, Vivian?" It was Troy Lang. He raised his hand to get her attention. Spirit hadn't seen Troy when she'd busted the boys out of prison; he must have been somewhere else in the building. "Spirit told us Doc A is really a crazy terrorist. Why don't we just go to the police instead of hiding here?"

Spirit saw Vivian sigh just a little. "As I'm sure Spirit said the *last* time you asked that question, the second thing that would happen would be that Mordred would wipe their memories, the way he's been wiping the memories of the people of Radial for years. And the first thing would be that he'd find us, and . . . Well, just think about what he's been doing to you so far, and imagine what he'll do to you if he catches you now. Come on. There isn't a lot of light left, and we're going to need it."

She gestured, and walked off. Troy and a few of the other boys followed. Spirit looked at Burke, her expression puzzled.

"Come on, come on," Burke said, smiling at her encouragingly. "I think I know what she's got in mind."

What Vivian had in mind was tents. When Spirit followed Burke around the back of the shack, she saw a huge half-ton truck painted Army green (she wondered if Vivian had stolen it; anything seemed possible). The entire back was filled with camping equipment. Soon Vivian had everyone hard at work putting up a tent city, unpacking sleeping bags, and inflating air mattresses.

"They're doing pretty well, for all the shocks they've gotten," Burke said to Spirit when they had a moment of privacy.

"Yes," she answered. "But I wish. . . . Burke, we didn't really do anything at Oakhurst except warn Mordred that we're still out here. While the Tree is intact, he's as powerful as ever."

"I know," Burke said quietly. "But it would be a lot harder to destroy the Tree if we were all dead."

The statement startled Spirit into a rueful laugh. "I guess you're right. Come on. Let's go see what we can do to help everyone settle in."

An hour later, there was an entire city of tents where there'd been nothing but broken ground and crumbling tarmac. There were even enough tents so that the four of them could sleep above ground as well. That was a relief—Spirit had never really gotten used to sleeping at the bottom of a hole in the ground. One of the tents had been designated as the medical tent (though the medical attention would be magical in nature), because a lot of the new arrivals were nursing sprains and bruises sustained in the escape.

Spirit knew she should go and tell Merlin what had happened today—though Vivian might have given him a preliminary report, Spirit supposed he'd want details—but Merlin was unlikely to cause a riot if he was ignored, and the refugees probably would. The longer everyone got to think about things, the less willing they were to cooperate.

"The one thing Oakhurst really didn't teach us was trust and cooperation," Burke muttered to Spirit, after he'd broken up yet another fight over supplies.

If there hadn't been a handful of natural leaders in the group, it would have been a lot worse, but Kelly, Dylan, Veronica, and Brenda rode herd on everyone with ruthless good humor, making and keeping order—and reminding them, over and over, that at least they weren't sealed into their rooms anymore.

When the tents were all up, everyone gathered in the center of the camp. Tents or no tents, it was clear Vivian hadn't really been expecting to have to deal with three dozen new residents, because she'd disappeared almost at once and was still nowhere to be seen.

"Listen up!" Burke said. "I know you all have a lot of questions, and I promise you, we'll do our best to answer them, but right now we need to make the area safe. Separate out into your Schools, and I'll take you around to the Wards and show you how they work."

Nobody moved.

"Who died and made you God?" a voice called from the back of the crowd. Spirit couldn't identify the voice. It might have been Brett Weber. For an instant she saw Burke's face transform with fury. She could almost hear the words he struggled not to speak. *Fools! You would deny the orders of your lawful lord?*

Yeah, that'd go over really well, Spirit thought wryly. But it was hard to remember to act like ordinary (ordinary for Oakhurst, anyway) teenagers, when they had the memories of being kings and queens. Even Loch—*Lancelot*—had been king in his own land before coming to Arthur's court. . . .

"School of Fire over here!" Kelly said, stepping out of the crowd and brandishing a glow stick. The tension of the moment was broken.

"Water here!" Dylan said, moving to stand beside her. Some of the attributions of Gifts to Schools didn't make a lot of sense on the surface: Jaunting, Dylan's Gift, belonged to the School of Water.

"Air!" Vanessa Cartwright said, her Georgia accent plain even in that one word. Van was an Air Mage, Spirit remembered now, with the root form of that School's Gift. She could call up a wind from nowhere, or suck all the air from a room with nothing more than a gesture.

"And Earth!" Loch said. Like a number of the students, Loch had minor Gifts from two schools, but Pathfinding was School of Earth.

With only a little grumbling, everyone sorted themselves into Schools. They followed Burke as he led them off to show them where the Wards were. In a few moments, the only ones there were Spirit—whose magic belonged to the Fifth School—and the four Radial kids, who weren't members of any School. Spirit knew from her own experience how off-balance and left out they must be feeling right now. Not just from all the high weirdness that had gone on today, but from being the only ones here without magic powers. She'd been in their place herself, and it really sucked.

"Come on, guys," Spirit said. "You're going to need to see this, too."

"Why?" Veronica Davenport said plaintively. "None of us has any magic. We're just people."

"*Normal* people," Brett muttered darkly.

"Sure," Spirit said brightly, ignoring Brett's tone of voice. "And being the only ones without magic isn't any fun—I know, I was at Oakhurst for six months as the only one there without it—but that doesn't mean you don't need to know where the Wards are. Mordred can track us with magic, but inside the Wards, he can't see us."

"You mean they're kind of like a force field?" Brenda asked.

Spirit smiled. "Kind of. The important thing is to stay inside them." She gestured, and they came with her reluctantly.

"But how are we going to know where they are?" Veronica asked.

"There's nothing magical about that part," Spirit said. "We marked them with chalk. It's a lot easier to just find a chalk mark than to hope you're in the right place, and not everybody has major magic."

That got her a wordless snort from Brett, but the four of them followed her willingly enough. The groups of Oakhurst students had each gathered at the Ward related to their School, and were deep in discussion. Spirit pretty much ignored them as she pointed out the boundaries of their campsite to the Radial teens. She already knew where the Wards and the boundaries were, and it was more important to keep the Townies from feeling that *all* magicians were their enemies. Oakhurst had set its students against each other as a matter of policy, and Mordred had nearly succeeded in claiming victory because of it.

"Do you think—I don't know—that other people have magic too?" Veronica asked wistfully.

I think it's something I wouldn't wish on my worst enemy, Spirit thought instantly, but she knew what Veronica was really asking.

"You're just hoping—" Juliette began.

"I don't know," Spirit said, cutting Juliette Weber off before she could say whatever cutting thing she was thinking of. "All I really know about magic is what they taught us up at Oakhurst. And I think there were plenty of lies mixed in to that."

It wasn't really an answer, but at least it stopped any further bickering. And for all Spirit knew, Veronica *did* have magic. Maybe Mordred hadn't cared about any magicians born in Radial. Maybe he hadn't bothered to check the kids there for magic powers. Maybe Veronica's magic was too faint for him to have seen. Spirit had no idea. And now wasn't the time to investigate.

153

That could wait until they found out whether the end of the world was going to actually happen.

After they all (Townies and magicians) had circled the camp and learned the boundaries, Vivian organized some of the Oakhurst students to help her bring up food from the pantry in the bunker. There were a couple of folding tables among the things in the truck, and when all the food was all set out, the campsite took on a weird picnic-y look. The Fire Witches were doing a good job of keeping the area warm, and the Oakhurst students began to split up into smaller groups. Spirit noticed that Veronica had joined one of them. She wondered if Veronica's question had been more urgent than she wanted Spirit to suspect. She'd managed to shake off Mordred's bespelling, after all. Maybe she really *was* another late-blooming magician.

"All we need to do now is build a campfire and we can sit around and sing songs," Addie murmured, walking up behind Spirit.

Spirit just shook her head. "If I'm supposed to be running this rebellion, I've got to say Princess Leia really never was my favorite."

"And so you think you suck at it," Addie said, with dismaying insight. "Well, nobody else would do any better, Spirit. And a lot of people would do worse."

Spirit just sighed. *Even if I could wave my hand and just make Mordred and Breakthrough vanish in a puff of smoke, we'd still have problems,* she thought in irritation. *There's all of us here, and we all have magic, and what if there are more magicians out there? What can we do about them? Anything?*

She wanted peace and quiet and a few minutes of not having to answer the same questions over and over again. She left Addie and retraced her steps until she was back at the invisible boundary. Only it wasn't that invisible now, since somebody'd gotten their hands on a can of bright orange spray-paint and not only marked each cardinal point but drawn a ragged circle on the tarmac to connect each one.

"It isn't easy, is it?" Burke asked, coming up quietly behind her.

"None of this is," Spirit answered bitterly. "Oh husband, would I had known my vow would bind all of us to eternal rebirth!" Spirit played back her own words in her head and hiccupped a little. "Um, that didn't exactly come out right," she muttered, blushing.

She could almost feel Burke smile in the darkness. "I got the gist of it. You—she—Guinevere—did the best she could at the time. And if we all weren't being reborn, then Mordred would have gotten out and nobody would have known what they were up against."

"But he wouldn't have had a candidate-pool to recruit his Shadow Knights from," Spirit answered inarguably. "That *geasa* of my invoking fell upon all of us, all the people of Britain, no matter who they'd fought for. I—*she*—shouldn't have done it."

"I disagree," Burke said. "But I'll be happy to argue it with you for years. After we win."

That made Spirit sputter out a strangled laugh. "You sound so certain we will!"

"It's one of those leadership skill things." She could tell Burke was choosing his words carefully, almost translating them from Old High Forsoothly-speak into modern-day English. "You act confident. You keep your doubts to yourself—or you only share them with people who won't spread them around."

"And *do* you have doubts?" Spirit asked daringly. This was in some ways a more intimate conversation than any she'd had with Burke ever before.

"I'd like to say I don't," Burke said. "But in fact, I'm not really sure what's going to happen now. I think we have a better chance of winning than it might look like, though."

"You're kidding, right?" Spirit said doubtfully.

"No." Burke shook his head. "Mordred's a. . . . A *control freak*," he said, and the words sounded strange, as if he really were translating them into Modern English (which he probably was). "He won't take anybody's advice. And we already know he isn't even trying to fit in to the modern world. He's trying to change it into what he knows. I figure that's going to set him up to make mistakes. Maybe critical ones. But that isn't why I came looking for you," he added apologetically.

"Oh?" Spirit asked. While his view of Mordred was encouraging, she wasn't sure how useful it was. What did it matter if Mordred made mistakes if he had the power to squash them like a bug?

"It's time for a council of war," Burke said.

Vivian was waiting for them in the Medical Tent. With her were Elizabeth, Loch and Addie, and a few of the others from Oakhurst: Dylan, Kelly, Troy, Vanessa, and Emily Davis.

Emily was about Spirit's own age, but Spirit didn't know her well. It wasn't just that Oakhurst didn't encourage friendships: Emily's Gift was Scrying, and the students who had it tended to keep to themselves even more than the usual run of student magicians.

"I've been talking to the people you rescued," Vivian said when they came in. "Trying to get an idea of what Mordred's doing, and how he's doing it. I know none of you think you saw or heard anything—" this was addressed to the Oakhurst students "—but you saw more than you know. And with Emily's help, I've gotten a good look at what's going on."

"So if you can see the future, are we going to win?" Loch said.

"Not the future," Vivian said. "The past and the present."

"Clairvoyance, not precognition," Vanessa said, after a moment's thought.

Vivian smiled slightly. "You'd be surprised how often getting a good look at the past is useful. But, moving on, the first thing you need to know is that not all the people who vanished—from Oakhurst and from Radial—did it because they were joining forces with the Black Snake. Mordred's started in on some heavy-duty necromancy in preparation for his conquest."

"Blood magic," Loch said in disgust.

"He's *sacrificing* them?" Dylan asked, his face twisted in revulsion.

"Yes," Vivian said. "Eventually, he would probably have killed everyone left at Oakhurst."

"But . . . why?" Spirit asked. Even her Reincarnate memories didn't contain much information on necromancy.

"The younger the victim, the more powerful the sacrifice," Vivian answered. "And he doesn't need any of them— *you*—now. He's got thirty years of Oakhurst graduates—all Shadow Knights—to draw on, and he knows who his main enemies are."

"He's gathered all the magicians at The Fortress," Elizabeth said, taking up the tale. "But he's not counting on just them to keep order. Ovcharenko was put in charge of hiring their foot soldiers, so right now there's a magical army of mercenaries in Radial."

"Those giants we fought today," Burke said slowly.

"I wonder if they're getting paid in T-shirts?" Loch asked irreverently.

"So," Vivian said. "That's what you have to deal with at The Fortress: Shadow Knights, monsters, and mercenaries."

"Do they all know what Mordred's going to do?" Spirit asked.

"The Shadow Knights and the monsters don't care—or at least, the Shadow Knights won't cross him, no matter what they might be thinking about his plans," Vivian said. "And the monsters can just go home again if they get tired of our world.

I suspect Mordred thinks the Shadow Knights will either fall into line completely—those who have their doubts—or if they don't, they'll provide more sacrifices for his blood magic."

"Lovely," Addie said with a sigh.

Kelly gave her an odd look. "I don't mean to be a wet blanket here, but you don't sound nearly upset enough for that news. I don't see how we can make him stop—and you've already said telling the authorities won't do any good."

"It won't," Spirit said firmly. "But we don't need to fight our way through an army. All we need to do is get to the oak tree in the Main Hall of Oakhurst. If we can destroy it, Mordred will be vulnerable. He may lose his magic completely. And without Mordred looking over his shoulder, Mark won't start the war."

Loch glanced at her, his face still. Spirit could read the unspoken words in his eyes. We hope Mark won't start the war with Mordred gone.

"Then haven't we won already?" Kelly asked. "I didn't exactly start a small fire today. Oakhurst and everything in it is toast. Game over."

"You started the fire on the top floor," Spirit pointed out. "Which, okay, I would have done the same thing. But it means their Water Witches probably managed to put it out before it reached the Main Hall. They know they need to protect the Tree from damage, even if they don't know why. That's why they were guarding it today when we went in."

"Then we just need to go back," Kelly said. "If we get a few of the other Fire Witches together, we should be able to turn Oakhurst into ashes pretty darned quick. As long as some-body evacuates it first."

"You don't even need to evacuate it," Troy said. "I'm not the only one here with Transmutation. School of Air is the most common school for guys."

Kelly nodded. "Fire and Water for girls, Earth and Air for guys, although anybody can have anything, really," she said, as if reciting a well-known lesson. "How many other Air Mages with Transmutation are here?"

"Not me," Vanessa said with a sigh. "Wish I did, but . . . no."

"I know Josh has it," Troy said. "And I think Noah or Colin. Maybe both. But if we go in and start turning everything from the roof on down into water, that will flood anyone out who's still there. That should take care of your evacuation."

"Leaving my team with the remains of a soaking wet man-sion to set on fire," Kelly said. "Thanks a lot, dude."

"But you can do it?" Spirit asked.

"Sure can," Kelly said. "Give us an hour and we'll give you a smoking hole in the ground." She grinned at Troy and high-fived him.

Burke and Loch looked at Spirit.

"Okay," she said. "I think it's a good plan. Tomorrow we'll go through everyone and see what Gifts everybody has. Then we can ask for volunteers. And go back to Oakhurst . . . better prepared." Because an Illusion Mage—another common Air Gift—could help them drive right up to Oakhurst almost un-noticed.

She tried not to think about Muirin, and failed.

"And as soon as Mordred is out of the picture," Addie said. "*Then* we call in the authorities."

*

I t was late that night before Spirit could actually do some-thing as mundane as sleep, and she still hadn't had time to go and talk to Merlin. She and the other three had been too busy keeping a lid on things.

It was Loch who'd pointed out that they had almost forty people here, and the longer the Oakhurst contingent got to think about things, the more they were likely to figure they had just as good an idea of what to do next as anyone else did—or to just decide that getting as far from Radial as they could before the missiles flew would be a really good idea. It was Burke who'd suggested they have everyone stand watches. It would give everyone something to do, and it would play into the core values (for definitions of values meaning just the opposite) that Oakhurst had instilled in them, because any-body on watch would probably rat out anybody who tried to sneak away. It was Addie who said they'd need to include the Radial kids in anything they did, because they were already "us-versus-them-ing" things enough without adding in wiz-ards versus Muggles. And Spirit had laughed bitterly and drawn up a watch list. Six people for each watch, and two hour watches (they really only needed two for a watch, but she suspected a lot of the people who signed up would bail, so it was good to have extras). That would mean only about half of them would have to stand a watch each night, so they could start with volunteers.

It went easier than she'd thought it would, but going around and getting everybody signed up meant yet another round of questions. Spirit knew why everyone kept asking the same questions over and over. It was because the answers were so unbelievable—and so *bad*—they kept hoping this time they'd be different. The idea that kindly old Dr. Ambrosius had murdered their families, that he'd been living a masquerade for decades while being some kind of movie villain mastermind, that he meant to destroy the world . . . those were all things it was hard to take seriously. Who'd want to believe in those truths, when they meant everyone at Oakhurst had lost their families not by some horrible accident, but by a murder that would never be prosecuted?

And the idea that the big plan now that they'd escaped and finally knew the truth about what was going on was for them to just sit here and not tell the authorities . . . well, Oakhurst hadn't been big on trust and cooperation, but one thing it had hammered home to all of them was submission to authority. And trying to understand that nobody in authority could help, well. . . . That was hard to accept.

So Spirit did the best she could to answer the (same old) questions, and to not sound as frustrated as she felt at having to. It was after midnight when she could finally stagger back to her tent to collapse, and half the tents were still lit up inside.

Maybe their inhabitants were just afraid of the dark.

God knew she would have been, if she'd found out all of this just today.

⁂

The flash of the cigarette lighter was bright in the darkness. Allan Tate didn't know where it had come from—even a book of matches was contraband at Oakhurst—but a moment later he caught the sweet scent of burning tobacco. Somebody was really going off the rez. He'd seen enough war movies— one of the few things he liked that weren't banned at Stalag Oakhurst—to know that sentries didn't smoke on duty (even if any of them had actually been old enough to smoke, except maybe that crazy lady who seemed to be in charge of this place). Lighting a cigarette screwed up your night vision. And the enemy could smell a cigarette from miles away and make your position.

Not that any of them were real sentries. And there probably wasn't a real enemy, either. All of this was just some kind of a game. Sort of.

Oh, he believed that everybody at Oakhurst was out to get them. But he sure didn't believe that Doc A was some kind of criminal mastermind. It was probably some kind of CIA or FBI or Homeland Security thing, where the government had finally found out about magic and wanted to get its hands on all of them.

Yeah. That was it. Forget about Breakthrough and all that crap Mark Rider was dishing out. Working for the Feds would be the real deal. Carry a gun, have everybody respect you. Probably get to have anything you wanted, because they'd know they needed you. It'd be cool. They'd want him particularly, because he was School of Air. All the best stuff was School of Air. Shadewalking, Animal Communication, Animal Control. . . .

And Illusion. That was better than all the others. And *he* had it.

It was one of the reasons he'd volunteered to stand guard. He figured that'd be a good way to get in with the inner circle here. Find out what was really going on. That way, when They made their move (whoever *They* were), he'd be in a position to negotiate. Maybe even dictate terms. Spirit had been smart to get them out of Oakhurst, sure. But she'd only been half smart. She'd been taken in by that dumb cover story. He was going to be all smart.

It was easy enough to cast an illusion that made him seem to vanish. He'd need to be quiet, because it would only mask sights, not sounds. But from the look of things, whoever was out here smoking wasn't going to be paying much attention.

Allan drifted closer. Now to see what they were up to. . . .

"Brett! What if they catch you?" Allan heard Juliette Weber clearly, even though she probably thought she was keeping her voice down.

"What're they going to do?" Brett Weber answered. "Kick me out?"

"No, but— And where did you get them, anyway?"

"Five-finger discount at that place we stopped at to use the rest rooms. You know, if I had magic like that girl does, I wouldn't waste it. I'd make myself a whole suitcase full of cash."

"Yeah? What if it wasn't real? You know—counterfeit."

Allan nodded approvingly. Juliette was pretty smart for a mundane. And pretty, too.

"Okay, gold and diamonds, then." Brett sounded irritated. "You know, none of this is really fair. Look at all the stuff that's happened to us—our whole town got erased—just because we're supposedly in the middle of this whole big supposed witch-war."

"But. . . . Spirit wasn't lying, Brett. You saw those things at the Library when Erika and Bella got killed. And . . . what happened at the Dance. They say Muirin's dead."

"So? Bella and Erika are dead, too. And probably Kennedy, the skank."

Allan heard Juliette snicker briefly. "Yeah," she said. "Nobody cares what happened to us."

"Yeah. Not then, and not now. So I figure we'd better be smart, and look out for oursel—*Hey!*"

There was the sound of a scuffle as Juliette snatched the cigarette away from Brett. Allan could see the two of them were standing at least three feet to the wrong side of the spray-painted line on the ground. He shrugged. They didn't have any magic. What could it matter?

"Yeah?" Juliette said suspiciously. "How? We're out here in the middle of nowhere. It's not like we can call our folks to come pick us up. . . . *Brett!* Do you think they're going to be okay?"

"Sure," Brett said, too quickly. "You heard what Spirit said. That guy wants to turn all of us into, like, medieval serfs. He needs them. And anyway, we can rescue them."

"How?" Juliette said, just as quickly. "Brett—"

"Look, Jule. All this talk about getting rid of this Mordred guy, that isn't going to work. If it would, they would've done it already. Isn't everybody saying there's no point in calling the cops or anything because he'll just fry their brains? If I'd known all that back in town, I wouldn't've left, and you wouldn't either. You want to spend a couple of weeks camping out in the middle of nowhere—and by the way, I didn't see any bathrooms—before we get rounded up and shot? I figure whatever he's doing, we should help him do it. If we do, I bet he'll be grateful and give us anything we want."

Allan sneered. *Idiots.* Doc A would be glad to get them all back, but if Brett Weber thought he'd be grateful to some small-town yahoo who didn't even have any magic. . . .

All I have to say is, I'd sure like to be there when Doc A turns Brett into a mouse. I bet he wouldn't turn him back, either.

He turned around and walked away, being careful to stay inside the Wards. Tomorrow morning he'd tell Spirit what he'd overheard. Or maybe Addie—it wasn't any secret she was some kind of big heiress. Then they could arrest the Webers—there had to be some place to lock them up around here—and then he'd have proven his loyalty. He figured that would give him the leverage to make his move. He glanced at his watch. Almost two a.m. The next shift would show up soon, and he didn't want them stealing his thunder.

He hunted around until he found a chunk of rock on the ground. *Nothing too big.* Then he took careful aim, and chucked it toward the Weber kids.

It bounced off the ground in front of them, and he heard Juliette yelp. But it did what he'd wanted it to. Juliette threw the cigarette out into the dark, and she and her brother moved back inside the boundary line.

⁂

Spirit didn't know why she woke up. One moment she was sound asleep, the next she was lying in bed, eyes open, noticing that the sky outside the tent was paling with dawn. That meant it was somewhere around seven a.m. She didn't really feel that six hours of sleep was enough, but in the last couple of weeks she'd gotten used to the idea that the day began with dawn. On the other side of the tent, she saw Burke turn over, and knew in another moment he'd be squirming out of his sleeping bag and getting ready to greet the day.

This would probably be a good time for her to finally go down into the bunker and talk to Merlin. Spirit knew she needed to check with him about what they were going to do next, but she hadn't wanted to do it when it was likely one of their guests would follow her down. Loch and Burke were right: their refugees were volatile. She hoped that if she could just—

Spirit never remembered later what she'd hoped for, because that's when the screaming started.

There was a half second when she couldn't identify the

meaning of the sound. That it was sound, yes. But that was all. And then it came clear, the way an image would when a page finished loading, and she was scrabbling for her sneakers, struggling out of her sleeping bag. For a few seconds more she hoped it was nothing worse than a bunch of the students trying to settle old feuds.

Then she heard the call of the hunting horn.

The Shadow Knights had found them.

Instinctively Spirit ran toward the sound, thinking of all the things she should have done. She should have put the people without combat magic together, made sure they knew where to run and hide. The four of them had been too confident yesterday, certain they'd escaped, certain the Wards would protect them.

Now they were all going to pay the price.

The pen became the Sword in her hand as she ran. Burke was on one side of her, Loch on the other. Addie (Spirit knew) was going to do whatever she could to help using the Cauldron.

She heard the clatter of hooves on asphalt. *That's insane,* Spirit thought wildly. *They can't have ridden here on horseback.* . . . But however they'd gotten here, she and the others were facing mounted Shadow Knights—and worse. There were a bunch of the giants they'd seen at Oakhurst. And other things. Things that should not be seen by the light of an April dawn.

It was chaos. She saw a couple of the horses go down—one

of the Water Witches had covered the ground with a sheet of ice. There were swirls of dust as Van and some of the other Air Mages made miniature tornadoes. Some people were fighting back.

But most of the kids just ran.

Spirit reached the foremost of the Shadow Knights, and swung her Sword. She acted out of instinct, but it didn't matter. Excalibur passed through the horse's body like smoke, and horse and rider disappeared.

Illusions! But not all of them are! And what do they want . . . ? It was not a question that Spirit White would have asked, but it was foremost in Guinevere's mind.

Ahead of her she saw Loch and Burke attack one of the giants. This time Loch didn't use his Spear as a club—he drove its point directly into the torso of his attacker. Spirit flinched, but a moment later she understood the reason for Loch's ruthless attack. The giant toppled with a crash, but the body that hit the ground wasn't flesh, but stone. Within seconds, it was nothing more than a jumble of boulders.

Spirit smelled smoke and spun around, looking back the way she'd come. *The tents! They're burning!* She didn't know whether their attackers had set them on fire, or some of the panicked Fire Witches, but the result was the same.

There's no cover out here—just a few broken-down shacks. We can't hold them off. We can't stop them. We have to get out of here.

"Come on!" she shouted, as loud as she could. "This way!"

She saw Burke's teeth flash as he nodded. He flung his fists out, and his Shield appeared, blocking a blow from a giant fist. Loch ducked under Burke's shield with Arondight, and another monster became unliving stone.

Spirit turned and ran toward the abandoned missile silo.

They'd all been trained to be soldiers at Oakhurst, Reincarnates or no. Several of the other kids had armed themselves with whatever they could find—those of them who weren't simply living weapons—and were sheltering in doorways and windows and against the broken remnants of walls.

The next thing seemed to happen in slow motion. She saw the bright brittle flare of sunlight on plate armor—a Shadow Knight, wearing whatever Mordred thought of as fancy dress the last time he'd been out and around—saw the horse gallop toward the shack that concealed the entrance to Merlin's bunker, saw the rider flourish, not a sword, but a bag in Army green, and she just had time to think *satchel bomb* as he reined in and threw.

But Spirit wasn't his target.

The bomb went past her, through the inner doorway, slid across the floor and over the rim of the hole in the floor. She saw that in a snapshot glimpse as she was turning and running. It didn't even matter that she was running *at* the Shadow Knight, so long as she was running away from the explosion to come. When it came, the ground jumped, and Spirit screamed in shock.

What came next was hazy and disjointed and fragmentary. As if it was coming from somewhere outside herself, Spirit heard herself shouting at everyone to get back to the bus.

People ran toward it, passing the word, doing sweeps to gather in the stragglers. If there was one thing they taught you to be good at, at Oakhurst, it was war. People ran for the bus while other people set up obstacles in the path of the Shadow Knights and their monstrous allies. Then Burke grabbed her up and tossed her through the open door of the bus, and Loch caught her, staggering, and Addie floored the accelerator, keeping the door open for Burke to chase them, catch them, and board.

The windows were darkened with mud and smoke, and even, in some places, covered in frost. Addie drove halfway by guess as her passengers screamed or cried or shouted, and Spirit, Loch, Burke, and Dylan staggered along the aisle trying to get an accurate count of survivors. There'd be time later to pick up the pieces, to assess the damage, to figure out what had happened and why they were all still alive.

"Somebody tell me where I'm going!" Addie shouted, her voice high and tight.

"Macalister!" It was Veronica Davenport. "Macalister High School—do you know where it is?"

"Right down the road from The Fortress," Loch said grimly.

"They won't go near it," Veronica said. "You can see it from the main highway. It's only about six hundred yards off it."

"And the Shadow Knights wouldn't want to attract attention by making it vanish overnight," Addie said in realization.

"Okay," Spirit said, before Burke could add anything. "It sounds good. Let's do it."

Burke looked at her in faint surprise. Guinevere had always let Arthur lead—or at least, let him be the public face of decisions they'd made jointly. But the more she'd deferred to him, the more Arthur had felt he needed to prove himself. To gain the position of leadership by right, and not as a gift.

It had made him reckless.

Not this time, Spirit thought. This time she wasn't taking a back seat to make things easier for people who couldn't handle the idea of everybody having opinions. And she knew Burke wouldn't want her to.

They were all on edge, expecting attack at any moment, but it didn't come. Finally Addie pulled the bus to a stop. "I can't stand it," she said. "Let's at least take a look."

Warily, the five of them—including Dylan—got out of the bus and looked back the way they'd come. It was a beautiful spring morning—except for the column of black smoke in the distance.

"Where'd they all *go?*" Dylan demanded.

"A better question is: where'd they come from?" Loch said. "Horses couldn't have covered the distance between Radial and the base in. . . . In the time between us busting you guys out of Oakhurst—Radial—and now."

"Not to mention, 'how did they find us?' " Burke said.

"That isn't as important as how we managed to escape," Spirit said pragmatically. "They had a lot of, well, supernatural creatures with them. For lack of a better word."

"But I don't think there were a lot of actual Shadow Knights," Loch said. "Most of the ones I saw were illusions."

"That explains why they left. But what did they *want?*" Addie asked.

"Can't you guess?" Spirit said bleakly. "They wanted Merlin. And they got him." *The Bad Guys threw a bomb down into the bunker, and blew up everything there, and now Merlin's dead.*

"But he's in the Internet," Loch said blankly.

Spirit didn't think it mattered. The Internet was so big that if a bomb ripped you loose from a specific IP address, you could search forever without finding that specific point ever again.

About a dozen kids hadn't made it onto the bus, and Spirit was pretty sure they'd vanished during the battle. Brett and Juliette Weber, Emily Davis—everyone, in fact, with the Scrying Gift, so Cassie Moore was gone too.

"Look on the bright side," Dylan said. "Even if they took prisoners, they can't get anything useful out of them. Nobody but us knows about the Reincarnates, and nobody knew where we were going to go."

They got back on the bus. There was nothing else to do.

SEVEN

Macalister High School served all of Macalister County, no matter where you lived: some of its students had a two-hour bus ride each way to get there (at least they had before the Spring Fling). When they got there, the school was deserted. Spirit had wondered where all the other teens were—since the school was deserted—until Veronica said the entire population of the county had been gathered into the village beneath The Fortress's walls.

"We all went to the Dance, we all ended up there," she said, shrugging. "And our folks, too."

Compared to the one at Oakhurst, the Macalister High gym was small and shabby, but it was still plenty large enough to hold everyone who'd been on the bus—and the bus, too. One advantage to having Reincarnate selves was that those of them who'd had magic in their other lives—mainly Addie—were now much better at it. The moment Addie had taken her "key ring" out of the ignition, it had reverted from a magic school bus to a decidedly non-magical black van. Addie had simply driven it inside. At least, Spirit hoped, it wouldn't attract the Shadow Knights' attention now.

"I think we'll be safe here," Loch said. "At least once we've put Wards up. And I think I've found out how the Shadow Knights found us, back at the silo," he added. He gestured toward one of the other students: Allan Tate, Spirit thought his name was. "Allan said Brett and Juliette were outside the Wards last night. Based on what he said, and what I'm guessing, Mordred had flying squads out searching for us, and they did enough to alert them."

"But why didn't they just kill us?" Spirit asked.

"Best guess?" Loch answered. "They didn't have detailed orders. And I don't think Mordred's the kind of guy you want to get creative on. So they did everything they could that was covered by their orders, and ran for reinforcements."

"Who should be *here* pretty soon," Spirit said wearily, "so if you've got any good ideas, now's the time."

She looked around the gym. Over near the bleachers, she could see that Burke was talking to everyone, organizing work parties and getting everyone to make lists of what they needed to settle in here. There'd been forty of them at the missile base. Now there were only thirty-two. Vivian was among the missing, and that hurt out of proportion to the loss. It seemed unfair for Vivian to have worked so hard and hidden so long and so successfully only to have fallen into Mordred's hands now. But at least Elizabeth was still among the survivors.

No, Guinevere whispered in Spirit's mind. *Iseult. And Gareth Beaumains, that noble knight. And more. . . .*

Spirit looked around the gym. Maybe her power had gotten stronger since she'd Awakened Dylan, or maybe now she just knew what she was looking for, because despite what Iseult had told her back when she was first telling Spirit about the Reincarnates, Spirit could not only tell which of them were Reincarnates—but who the Reincarnates were. And what she saw—scattered among the Oakhurst refugees—were Guinevere's friends, vassals, comrades. She saw her friends— but she also saw Arthur, Lancelot, Vivianne. . . .

Here were Gareth and Iseult, who were also Dylan Williams and Elizabeth Walker. There was Brangane, the sorceress who'd aided Iseult—in this life Maddie Harris—and Bertilak, the Green Knight's warrior bride—Kylee Williamson. Cei and Bedivere, Dagonet and Morholt, Olwen, Peredur, Laudine, Loholt . . . and Gaheris, Gareth's brother.

And Agravaine's brother, too. Dylan-slash-Gareth had come down on their side. Would Chris Terry make the same choice if she awakened his Reincarnate self? Or would he side with his other "brother"—and the Shadow Knights?

No, Spirit thought. *I have to believe Chris—Gaheris—is a Grail Knight, not a Shadow Knight. That's why they locked him up. . . .*

In a way, Mordred had done the selection of Spirit's allies

for her. And with a dozen Reincarnates, and a dozen magicians, surely they could do . . . something?

"First things first," Burke said, coming over to them. "Let's make sure the Black Snake can't find us."

✤

urke's plan was elegant. (And, Spirit thought, it had a chance of actually working.) Thanks to Veronica, they knew that there was a bomb shelter in the basement—the school dated from the 1950s—which had been converted to an emergency shelter. It was full of cots, blankets, and cases of MREs.

"Continuing our Cold War motif," Loch said grandly, as he opened the door. "We present—an actual Atomic Bomb Shelter!"

"It's for bad weather, mainly," Brenda Copeland said, walking past him to flip the light switch. Nothing happened, and she made a face. "We lose power a lot around here in the winter, and when that happens, folks need a place to go so they don't freeze. The school's got an emergency generator, too, but I don't guess we'll be firing it up any day soon."

"Yeah," Loch said. "How about not?"

Spirit suddenly realized that while people had been shivering down here during the winter blizzards, Oakhurst had probably had not only its own power plant (both mundane and magical) but enough space that it could take in everyone in Radial without anyone being cramped. (If it hadn't been a fortress being run by an insane necromancer, of course.) She

177

wondered if this shelter had been needed in the years since Oakhurst had opened—and if so, how often. And at the same time, another part of her was thinking that Mordred was no true lord and knight, to refuse the shelter of his castle to townsfolk in need.

She wondered if this kind of "double vision" was as confusing to the other Awakened Reincarnates as it was to her.

"We'll hide the van under the bleachers in the gym," Burke said, "and Angela can show the rest of the Air Mages how to sweep away every trace that shows we're here. Then we hunker down here in the basement, and Ward the heck out of it."

"So the atomic bomb shelter becomes a magical bomb shelter," Loch said.

Burke nodded. "They can stomp around the school until the cows come home. But they won't find us down here. And I'm going to bet that if they search it once, they won't bother to search it twice."

"Great," Spirit said, trying to force enthusiasm into her voice that she didn't feel.

She didn't ask what they'd do next.

She knew the answer.

*

*N*ervous energy carried everyone through all their preparations. The shelter was large enough for all of them—Veronica said it was rated for fifty—though when all the cots were set up it would be a little hard to move around.

Spirit realized that it hardly mattered whether Merlin was

still out there on the Internet or not—the school had a few computers for student use, and one of them even connected to the Internet (Veronica said)—but without electricity, they might as well just be so many big chunks of plastic. Whether Merlin was out there or not, they were on their own now.

Angela and Kylee did the sweep of the school—everywhere inside it any of them had been, and around the outside, too—with Allan going along to help hide them while they did it. As far as Spirit could understand, it was kind of like casting a set of inside-out Wards: you weren't building an impenetrable wall that nothing could get through. You were sweeping away everything that a Warding might hide.

Once they were all inside the shelter, Burke went around chalking marks on the walls and the floor. Then he lifted Loch up to do the same on the ceiling.

"Is that it?" Brenda asked, when he was done. She sounded puzzled and a little disappointed. Burke smiled at her.

"Just the start. Benchmarks, you might say. Now we turn them into protection," Loch answered.

Spirit knew, from the few things Addie and Muirin had said (and oh, god, would there ever be a time when she could think of Muirin without tears?) that setting Wards was advanced magic that wasn't taught until the very end of your time at Oakhurst—undoubtedly set up that way so the Oakhurst students couldn't hide things from their teachers (assuming, of course, she thought, anyone ever really *did* graduate from Hellmouth Academy). All anyone was usually taught before then was how to recognize Wards and make them stronger. Creating them was a different thing. Of everyone here, only Addie had the knowledge to do that. The Lady of the Lake was a powerful sorceress in her own right, even without the power of the Hallows.

So six times Addie—*Vivianne*—created the fragile scaffold of the Warding, and six times the young magicians filled them with power—the power not of four Schools, but five. Spirit—Guinevere—felt herself at the center of a vortex of raw power, once again at one with the land, as she had been when she had held the power of Britain in her Gift. As she had three times before in this lifetime, she let herself serve as a conduit of the great force of Life and Light, channeling it into the friends and comrades around her, molding their power into something vast and good.

A sword against the Darkness.

It seemed to Spirit she could hear a high bell-like chime when the sixth Ward snapped into place with the other five. *Just let them try to see through that!* she thought in fierce triumph.

"Whoa," Blake Watson said, gazing down at his hands as if he expected to see his palms smoking. "That was intense."

Spirit hid a smile as she looked at the Radial kids. Brenda was looking puzzled, as if she'd gone to a concert and there'd been only silence. Veronica was looking hopeful, as if she might be able to hear the music if she only tried hard enough.

"Did you really do anything?" Veronica blurted out, and then blushed furiously.

"I didn't see anything," Brenda said doubtfully. "You just all stood around staring at each other for a couple of minutes."

"Indeed," Dylan said. "We did a parlous thing. And now we can rest easy—chill out—here in our nice warm bunker."

Spirit recognized the signs of Dylan editing his speech to cut out the worst of Gareth's forsoothlyness and tried not to grimace. It was hard enough to be a teen wizard. It was a lot worse when you also had the memories of somebody years older than you were who'd lived centuries ago. And who, in a sense, *was* you.

"We're safe, for now," Burke said. "So I guess it's time to make plans."

There was really only one possible plan. The question was: how? The Oakhurst students simply assumed they were going to fight—it was what they'd been trained for, after all. And whether they wanted to just run away or not, Oakhurst had carefully taught them—month after month, year after year—that escape was impossible.

If they couldn't run, they had to fight. And their deadline—May First—was getting closer every hour.

Burke organized their forces. Everyone knew him, and everyone liked him—he'd been at Oakhurst longer than anyone else in their rebel band. On the morning after their arrival, Burke sent out scouting parties—Shadewalkers and Illusion Mages, who could move about the area without being seen. His aim wasn't to have them enter the enemy camp—one magician could sense another if they were using their

Gift—but to see if the Shadow Knights were hunting them, or coming toward the school, and to gather any other information they could.

Of the thirty magicians in their group, five had the requisite Gifts. There were two Shadewalkers, Loch and another boy named Russell Frazier, and three Illusion Mages: Renee Trueblood, Mike Sherwood, and Allan Tate. Spirit knew that Loch could protect himself, but of the others, only Allan was a Reincarnate (but an unAwakened one, for what that was worth), and Renee was only thirteen. She was the youngest. Of all the kids here, Angelina Swanson, eighteen, was the oldest.

Most of us aren't even old enough to vote, and we've got to save the world.

"I don't get it," Brenda said, puzzled.

The two Radial teens were, Spirit knew, valuable allies, and she'd made sure to tell them so, and include them in both the planning and in things as minor as being there when they opened the door of the gym to let their scouting party out. Neither one had magic, so neither one could be influenced by a lot of the subtle spells Mordred might cast to make them reveal themselves. And to a magical search, they would be invisible.

Brenda glanced at Spirit. "You're all kids, like us. And they're just going to . . . walk out there? Without even, I don't know, a Kevlar vest or anything?"

"Kevlar's hot, and mail is hot, noisy, and heavy," Loch said, absently. He was bundled up in several sweaters against the cold, because the heavy canvas parka Vivian had given him would rustle when he moved. He was checking himself over carefully: making sure he was wearing nothing that would reflect light, or catch on something, or make noise when he moved. He glanced up at Brenda and smiled. "Yeah, we are. And it's not just because we don't have a real choice. It's because we've trained to do this. Say what you will about Oakhurst—and I could say quite a lot—it trained us to fight. And now we're going to."

He opened the door just far enough to slip out. Spirit watched after him, then blinked, realizing she couldn't see him any longer.

"Was that magic?" Veronica asked. "Can you still see him?"

"Yes, it was," Spirit said. "And no, I can't. It's complicated."

"I can," Russ Frazier said, grinning. He was another Shadewalker, after all. "My turn."

He slipped out the door, and one by one, the three Illusion Mages followed. Then all there was left to do was wait. Some people stayed down in the basement. Some came up to the first floor to look around. Others went picking through the athletic equipment stored here, looking for things that could be made into weapons. The Cauldron could transform anything placed into it into what you needed it to be, but the closer it was to what you wanted it to be to begin with, the easier the transformation was. And if your Gift allowed you to turn wood to stone—or to iron—even a hockey stick could become a deadly weapon.

verybody was on edge until the five scouts returned from their first reconnaissance. They were able to report that there was no sign of activity east of The Fortress—that was the side Macalister High was on. Twenty miles west stood the old Tyniger Manor: Oakhurst Academy.

"No Wards," Allan Tate said. "And no search parties, either. Or any kind of guards."

"What could they possibly need to guard?" Loch sniped. "They've brainwashed an entire town into thinking they're medieval peasants, and everyone in The Fortress has gone over to the Dark Side."

Russ Frazier and Mike Sherwood reported much the same thing—if anybody was out looking for them, they weren't doing it from horseback or in cars. "Not that there's anything like a road left once you get far enough away from the high school," Mike said, with a shrug.

"So they aren't going to keep looking for you?" Brenda asked. "After all they did—following you to Nebraska, attacking you, *killing* people—they're just going to forget about you?" She sounded both baffled and indignant.

"They probably think we're still running," Loch said.

"We aren't their priority," Burke said (and oh, it was Arthur that Spirit heard in his voice, Arthur who had grown to manhood waging war while dreaming always of peace). "And they don't think we're a major threat. At least Mordred doesn't think so. And he's the one calling the shots—woe betide any wight who exceeds his authority. Er, as it were. I think they'll keep looking for us, but they'll be looking in Nebraska, and that's a bit of a hike from their home base. We'll have a few days' grace, I think, before they really start looking closer to home."

They had the Cauldron's magic to thank for that, Spirit/Guinevere knew. There would be no trail for Mordred's hunters to follow back here to find them.

"I saw something out there," Renee said, shivering. "At least I think I did."

"Ah, but did it see you?" Addie's voice held all of Vivianne's authority and her assumption of rule. "It can't have, or we'd all be dead now." She smiled encouragingly at Renee.

Way to make everybody feel better, Spirit thought, and felt her other self smile in rueful agreement.

"So we aren't dead and what was it?" Dylan demanded. He, too, was having trouble sorting his Reincarnate self out from his present life; he spoke as if he were used to commanding instant obedience.

"I don't know for sure," Renee said. Her jaw firmed. It was far too old an expression for her face. "If I thought it'd seen me, I wouldn't have come back here," she said flatly. "But—School of Air, Illusion, you know the drill—I can see right through them. And there was a stand of trees, right at the edge of where the road is turned to grass."

"County's been talking about cutting those down since forever," Brenda said quietly.

"So it was bespelled," Renee said. "Only, under the illusion, it was still trees, okay? Only. . . . I think they were alive."

"Alive like . . . ?" Spirit prompted carefully.

"Like in that *movie!*" Renee burst out. "Where the trees were people, and they walked around."

"Ent, misbehaving," Loch said, and the sheer magnitude of that horrible pun was enough to make Addie groan and Spirit roll her eyes.

"Maybe that's what Mordred's using for sentries," Burke said after a moment's thought. "It'd make sense."

"I'm going to guess that from now on, saying the hills are alive isn't going to be funny," Allan Tate said.

"Not even a little bit," Loch answered.

❋

They were going to make a last stand against The Forces of Darkness™, and the idea was so insane that even Guinevere, who had faced down Mordred's dark army the first time, found it implausible. But they had no choice. Eventually the Shadow Knights would search Macalister High and find them. Or they'd just tear it down, and find them that way. Or Mordred would launch the missiles. Before any of those things happened—*instead* of any of those things happening—they had to defeat the Shadow Knights. Which meant defeating Mordred first. Which meant burning the Oak to ash.

That had to be their first priority. Nothing else would have much point if they couldn't destroy the source of Mordred's power.

And for that reason, Spirit's target wasn't The Fortress. There was no way they could storm that with just them, no matter how powerful their magic might be. But Loch had confirmed that Oakhurst was still standing (though the upper stories were burnt out and the roof had fallen in), and so she meant to strike at the Gallows Oak. It might not be the source of Mordred's power, but it was clearly his weak spot. Leave it intact, and he might be able to jump to a new body. Destroy the Oak, and they might have a chance against the Shadow Knights.

"I don't think Mark really wants to rule over a post-atomic wasteland," Spirit said to Burke. "But I'm not sure how we can use that."

"Any indecision on the part of the foe is a weakness his attacker can exploit," Burke said. She saw him grimace as he heard his own words—they were Arthur's, not Burke's.

It was evening, and they'd snatched a moment of privacy by offering to do the last sweep through the gym. Everyone else was already down in the shelter.

How often had she and Arthur snatched just such moments of privacy at the edge of his war camp?

Spirit shook her head, trying to remember . . . *what?* She didn't know. Spirit White, of Flat Rock, Indiana? Her parents? Her sister? That life seemed unreal now. She was Guinevere of Britain, *Bán Steud,* daughter of the White Mare.

"I never liked those movies anyway," Burke said, idly. "And I'm willing to bet Mark didn't either. Teddy probably did, though. . . ." He took a deep breath. "I know this is a fell unchancy thing, my lady, that neither you nor I did ever hope to see." He took a deep breath. "And this is just as weird for me as it is for you. Honest."

She smiled, just a little. "I wish. . . ." She stopped. She wasn't sure what she wished for. To be Guinevere, and not remember having been Spirit? To just be Spirit, without the memory of a whole other life—and love—crowding her brain? "I wish we didn't have to fight the forces of evil," she said finally.

"I hope . . ." Burke's voice trailed off. "I hope this battle will be an end to it," he said.

Spirit shuddered. The thought that she might die was both terrifying and unreal. The thought that *Guinevere* would have to be born again because Mordred was still around . . . that was a fear real enough to make her shake. When Guinevere was born again—*if* she was—and if she remembered herself again, she wouldn't remember having been Spirit White. Spirit knew Guinevere must have been born over and over since Mordred had been sealed in the Tree. But she didn't remember any of those lives or deaths.

Our life is but a brief candle, lighting our way between darkness and darkness, the ghostly voice of her other self whispered in her mind. *It leaves behind it no trace. And yet . . . I would lay down this burden if I could.*

So would I, Spirit thought.

"Well, soon enough we'll know," she said, putting on a show of comic bravado to make Burke smile. "Come on. Let's go see what's yummy in MRE-land."

"Nothing," Burke said fervently, and squeezed her hand.

"And I hope you're right. About Mark, I mean. Because blowing up the world is a real deal-breaker."

✦

I t took them a week to make their preparations. Transmutation turned basic sports equipment to stone or metal, and Vivianne conjured the transmuted items into true spears and swords—and armor.

The last thing they meant to do would be the most dangerous, because it was the most likely to attract attention. For the trip to Oakhurst, they would need horses. Addie couldn't drive a school bus over the muddy terrain between here and Oakhurst, and the sound of its engine was something no spell of Illusion could cloak. So just before they left, those with Animal Control or Animal Communication would summon horses. The scouts had seen horses running loose, and even if there were stables inside The Fortress, there weren't enough for all the horses around here—both the ones from Oakhurst, and the ones some of the kids in Radial had had. So they'd call the horses. And mount. And ride out. And Addie would bring Brenda and Veronica in the van, following the riders as well as she could. At least somebody would be out of the battlefield. And maybe—if this didn't work—the three of them could actually manage to warn someone before Mordred brought the world to an end.

Only if that had any chance of working, it would have been Plan A instead of being somewhere down around Plan Q.

All too soon, their attack wasn't days away, but only an

hour or two at most. They'd spent the afternoon putting blankets up over all the windows, and if any light showed through, well, it would be candlelight, and not as likely to attract attention.

The gym was a quiet hive of activity, lit by the flickering light of the emergency candles from the shelter. Everyone was checking their armor and weapons with grim concentration. Spirit knew that most of them weren't really sure about what they were about to do—or to be more accurate, about why they were doing it, aside from taking the chance to strike back at the people who had persecuted them for so long. But one thing Oakhurst had excelled at was turning them into warriors.

"Take a walk with me?" Burke asked, coming up to where Spirit sat, nervously twirling the pen, her disguised Hallow, between her fingers.

She glanced up. Football padding and a heavy sweater had become armor and chain mail. He looked both more and less like the man her Reincarnate memories told her he was. "Sure," she said, getting to her feet.

To her surprise, he led her outside. The sky was cloudless, but the stars weren't the bright bitter stars of winter. It was spring, and the air had a fugitive hint of warmth. She looked up, taking a moment to admire the beauty of the night sky. It seemed as if every day since the Spring Fling, she'd been saying goodbye. Goodbye to the sunrise, to the sunset, to cheap fast-food hamburgers, to Coca-Cola. *Goodbye, goodbye, goodbye.* Everything around her seemed painfully real—and painfully short-lived—as if she had to notice them, pay attention to them, because it would be the last time she would see any of them. It didn't matter whether it was wonderful—snowdrops by the side of the road, the haze of new leaves on the trees—or not so wonderful—scratchy blankets, a damp basement, bad food— she was having each experience for the last time.

Soon would come the last time she ever saw Burke.

No! she shouted inside her mind. *I won't think that way! We'll win!*

She knew she'd try her best. They all would. But knowing that did nothing to change the sense that she was bidding the world a long farewell.

"I figure they'll start Calling the horses soon," Burke said, breaking into her thoughts. "After that, if somebody's going to notice us, we'll be noticed," he said. "There's nothing we can do about it one way or the other. But I wanted to talk to you first."

Spirit glanced up at him in puzzlement. They had no good-byes to say to each other—it was ill luck before a battle. "What about?" she asked.

"I know what you can do," Burke said. "You did it to Dylan. You need to do it to the others—I know some of us must be Reincarnates, and I think you can see who. Waken their memories. Now. Before we fight."

"I—" Cravenly, she'd hoped he'd forgotten what she'd done before. She knew she could call the Grail Knights to awareness, just as Mordred could call the Shadow Knights. It was the one thing she and Mordred shared: the bodies they wore in this life were both magicians whose Gift was of the School of Spirit. It was why, she supposed, Mordred had been able to take Kenneth Hawking's body for his own. And why she'd been able to see through the web of glamourie he'd woven around Oakhurst and all it contained. But as often as she'd considered waking the memories of the other Reincarnates, Spirit, if not Guinevere, had rejected the idea. Tried not to think about it. "Burke. . . ." she said, and stopped. She didn't know what words came next.

Burke was waiting for her answer. He would wait, she knew, as long as he had to for her to give it.

"Elizabeth said that she, Elizabeth, didn't exist," Spirit began in a low voice. "She said she'd never existed, that Elizabeth Walker was nothing but a dream Iseult of Cornwall had dreamed—and awoke from. And you know, at the time I thought she was just crazy. But now I know she's right. Spirit White doesn't exist. Neither does Burke Hallows. Or Lachlan Spears. Or Adelaide Lake. There's only Guinevere and Arthur, Lancelot and Vivianne. And I can barely deal with that, and Addie. . . . I don't think Addie's *there* any more. I think Vivianne has forgotten Addie. We might die today. Some of us probably will die, and it doesn't matter if I, Guinevere, have seen it a thousand times before. It still scares me. It's still death. And how can I take away. . . ." She paused, swallowing hard. "How can I take away their last moments of life by turning them into someone else?"

"You must, my lady." There was nothing of Burke in his voice now. "This is the battle we have all pledged our souls to fight. The battle we bound our spirits to an endless rebirth to wage. Do you think I rejoice to have been denied Heaven? To wander the earth like a hungry ghost, century after century, denied both rest and my true name? And yet, it is a yoke I willingly bend my neck to, for I pledged to be a strong shield between the land and its enemies."

"Even if it's Montana and not Britain?" she asked, desperately hoping to sway him. *This isn't our fight—not Arthur's and Guinevere's—it's theirs. . . .*

"Even so," Arthur answered. "And I pledged my life and my soul gladly to this task. So did we all. You do not have the right to choose this for them, this oblivion and forgetting. After all this time, our friends, our allies, deserve the right to ride into battle knowing who they face, and what—and *why*. And . . . they are our sworn vassals, my Queen. Blooded knights and mighty sorceresses. Their memories—their skills—may be all that save us."

"But if we win?" Guinevere said urgently. "Arthur—if we win—what becomes of us?"

That was the fear behind all the others. Not of defeat, but of *victory*—of facing all the years this strong young body might live knowing herself nothing more than a ghost out of time. Fitting into the world around her as poorly as Mordred himself did. Yearning always for a land and a time lost beneath the crashing waves of centuries.

"It doesn't matter," Arthur said heavily. "I cannot allow it to matter. I am sworn to give my life for the land, and in life and death, my word is the same: I serve. I cannot order this, my lady. But I can ask it. Give your people the chance to knowingly redeem their oaths."

She bowed her head. Spirit, Guinevere, who she was and who she'd been was nothing but confusion in her mind now. All that was left was the promise she'd made so very long ago.

"Come, beloved," she said heavily. "Let us go inside."

❀

She looked around the gymnasium. Among the students who'd survived the attack on Merlin's base there were a dozen Reincarnates who had not yet been Awakened. It would be cruel to do it in front of everybody.

It would be cruel to do it at all. But Arthur was right.

She walked over to Maddie Harris. Maddie had been Queen of the Ditzes at Oakhurst, legendary for hitting "Reply All" on her e-mails and sending the entire student body blow-by-blow accounts of Dance Committee infighting. *In this life only*, Guinevere whispered in Spirit's mind. No one could have survived at Oakhurst as long as she had without being more than that. Now that disaster had well and truly struck, Maddie had dropped the over-the-top hysterics and end-of-the-world posturing. Spirit supposed it had been protective coloration in its way, for Guinevere knew her as Brangane, the confidante of Iseult of Cornwall, a woman whose sorcerous power had rivaled that of her mistress.

"Maddie?" she said. "Could you come out into the hall with me for just a second?"

Maddie frowned, but set aside the sword whose steel blade

she was sharpening and got to her feet. "Sure," she said. "What's up?"

"Just a few last-minute things," Spirit said. She pushed open the doors that led from the gym into the school. "There's something I need you to do before we leave today."

"What?" Maddie asked.

Spirit reached out and took both of Maddie's hands in hers. "I need you to *wake up*."

She felt the power uncoil within her, flowing from her hands into Maddie's. She saw Maddie blink in confusion, then watched her eyes grow wide with the knowledge of a life Maddie Harris had never lived.

It was over very quickly.

It felt like a death.

"My queen!" Brangane gasped. She started to curtsey, then caught herself. "Oh my god. . . ." she whispered, now sounding like Maddie.

"I'm sorry," Spirit said helplessly. "Iseult is here," she said. "Go to her."

Brangane withdrew her hands from Spirit's and stepped away. "Thank you," she whispered.

Spirit waited a moment longer, then went out into the gym to fetch another Reincarnate.

Dagonet had been Arthur's Court Fool, the only one licensed by law and custom to speak truths the King might not wish to hear. Dagonet had also borne another title: he had been the master of Arthur's spies. It seemed oddly fitting that in this life he was Allan Tate, Illusion Mage.

"You should have done this sooner, my lady," he said the moment he'd been Awakened. "For now you must ride into battle without any goodly rede of mine."

"I will not cry your pardon for keeping mine own counsel," Guinevere answered him tartly. "Would you have done any differently than I?"

Dagonet smiled. "You have done no other than I would myself have done. Now bide you here, and I shall send you another brave spirit to waken to battle."

I suppose that will work better than me going to drag people off one by one, Spirit thought to herself wearily.

A few moments later, Noah Turner walked through the doors. Noah Turner had been Cei, who had been raised beside Arthur in the halls of that lonely northern castle where Arthur had gone to be trained in all the arts of war. "Allan said you wanted to tell me something?" he asked doubtfully.

He stared at her in confusion when she awoke his true self, and fled back into the gym without a single word. The door had barely finished swinging back when Chris Terry pushed it open.

"I, uh. . . . I guess I'm one of Arthur's court?" he said uncertainly. He smiled at the look on her face. "I mean, it's not like you could keep what you're doing in here a secret. And you guys have all been acting weird since you came back. So. . . . I'm in. Only. . . . do you know . . . ?"

"Who you were before this life?" Spirit finished gently. "You were my noble knight, Gaheris of Orkney. And I'm sorry to have to break the news to you, but Dylan's your brother."

Chris laughed. "I guess I can deal with that. Just . . . is it going to hurt? Like when Doc A tested us?"

"No," Spirit said. She held out her hands. "It doesn't hurt."

* * *

Kylee Williamson burst into tears when she regained her Reincarnate memories. She was the Reincarnate Bertilak, and Bertilak had been the wife of the Green Knight. And Beckett Green—the Green Knight—was dead.

Blake Watson breathed a sigh of relief when he knew he had once been Peredur, one of The Merlin's knightly escort. "I'd been afraid I wouldn't be brave enough to fight," he said in a low voice. "Now I know I can. Thank you."

It didn't take long. When the last of the Reincarnates had been Awakened—Andrew Hayes, Fire Witch, became Bedivere, who had once held the fire of the Grail in his bare hands—Guinevere walked back out into the gym.

Seventeen of them were Grail Knights. Thirteen were Oakhurst's student magicians. And two were the people they were doing all this for—but it was their fight, too.

"What about the rest of us?" Angelina asked.

Spirit looked around the room. The Grail Knights all stood together. Brenda and Veronica stood at the edge of the non-Reincarnates, looking a little lost.

"The rest of you are just going to have to settle for being fabulous," Spirit said. It was as if Muirin stood at her shoulder, whispering the words into her ear. There was scattered laughter. "Remember, just being you, you survived everything that

Oakhurst and Breakthrough could throw at us. This doesn't change anything. Breakthrough is still going to start a war, and we still have to stop it."

"If it doesn't matter—" Troy Lang began.

Then why did you do it? Spirit heard the unspoken words as clearly as if they'd been said aloud.

"No. She's right." Kelly Langley—who wasn't a Reincarnate—stepped forward and turned to face the crowd. "This doesn't change anything. Maybe you think it's glamorous to be turned into somebody else. But there's nothing glamorous about what we're going out there to do. It's going to be messy, and a lot of us are going to get hurt. I'm glad to still be me. And I'm also glad we have some experienced dragon-slaying help. And I am going to *kick ass!*"

This time, everyone cheered.

EIGHT

When it was still an hour before dawn, they opened the doors of the gym and pushed the black van out into the yard by hand, so that the sound of its engine wouldn't alert any listeners. The Air Mages with Animal Communication and Animal Control began summoning horses, and Troy turned the basketball court from blacktop to turf.

At the very last minute, Gaheris worked a spell to fill the morning air with a thick, dense, impenetrable fog. The horses that had been summoned came silently through the mist, like ghosts, and stood patiently waiting to be saddled.

"Hey, who's this guy?" Molly Piercy asked. She was one of the Air Mages who'd helped call the loose horses. She patted the shoulder of a horse none of them had ever seen before. The animals the Oakhurst students had practiced Endurance

Riding on were all chestnuts or bays—this one was so white he nearly glowed.

"He's not from anywhere around Radial," Brenda said. "I know everybody's horses from the county."

"And the Shadow Knights' horses are all black," Kelley said. "Okay, who wants to be a target?" They all knew that the reason commanders from the old days used to ride white horses into battle was because they could be seen for miles. Their riders were automatically targets.

"I think he's here for me," Spirit said. She walked up to him and stroked his nose. "Hello, Passelande. It's been a long time."

The White Horse of Britain nodded his head up and down as if he understood, and she leaned against him for a moment, savoring the warmth and the familiar scent of horse.

"All of our old friends have come," Burke said, coming to her through the mist. At his side walked an enormous white hound. It looked a little like a wolfhound, and a lot like something nobody had ever seen before.

"Cafall!" Spirit said in delight. "Where did you come from?"

Cafall—Arthur's hound—shoved his wet nose into her hand. She scratched his ears.

"From the same place Passelande and all the rest came from," Burke said, stroking Cafall's head as well. "Because Mordred is loosed, and the last battle is to be fought."

"The Palug Cat, and the Green Knight, and the Boar of Triath," Spirit said. "They all stand now, with us—or against us." Arthur's Court had been a place not entirely of the world

200

in which they now stood, and creatures of Otherrealm had moved as freely through it as the men and women of Britain.

"It's a good omen," Burke answered. "Are you ready?"

"I am," she answered. He made a stirrup of his hand and tossed her up onto Passelande's back. She didn't need saddle or bridle to ride this horse.

All too quickly, it seemed, their mounts were ready. Burke rode beside her on Hengroen, another of the White Horses of Britain, of whom it had been said that he was swift enough to outrace the sun and the moon together.

And now we ride to battle, the ghostly voice whispered in her mind.

❦

Shrouded in illusions and blanketed by mist, the war party circled wide around The Fortress and the peasant village that lay at its foot. Spirit and Burke led them, but behind the two of them (she was glad to see it) Oakhurst mages and Reincarnate knights mingled freely. She gripped the hilt of her Hallow tightly, as if it might disappear if she didn't. The weight of the sword blade was heavy across her thighs. *I should have asked Vivianne to make a scabbard for me,* she thought absently. The sword's true scabbard had been as magical as Excalibur itself. But Mordred had destroyed it long ago.

It seemed as if they rode through a landscape as deserted as the one Mordred meant to make. After a few minutes, Loch rode up to them, his Spear in his hand, and took the lead. His Pathfinder Gifts could lead them to Oakhurst even through the fog. Dawn turned the mist first to gold, then to white, then the sun burned it away as they rode westward, and when it was gone, Spirit could see they were a few miles past the edge of the village. She urged Passelande into a ground-eating trot.

It seemed strange to ride as if she were an outlaw, without banners flapping in the wind, without bright gilded armor and bright surcoats blazoned with the devices that identified their wearers. Spirit shook her head, trying to get rid of the strange double-vision of Guinevere's memories. If they were lucky, they could win the battle today without striking a single blow.

But of course, they were never lucky.

The spur road that ran through Radial and then connected up with the Interstate used to run past the gates of Oakhurst, but now there was nothing there but grass. Their horses vaulted the low wall at the foot of the hill and galloped up the slope. Spirit heard yelps of glee from behind her as some of the riders forgot themselves in the excitement of the jump. Ahead she could see the main building of what had once been the school. Just as the scouts had said, the roof was gone, and the upper stories were smoke-blackened and half-ruined from the fire Kelly had set only a little more than a week ago to cover their escape. But the first floor—and the Great Hall—seemed to be intact.

Spirit vaulted from Passelande's back and ran up the steps, Excalibur flashing in her hand. In that moment she was Guine-vere and no one else—Guinevere who meant to put an end to

Mordred and the dark centuries of plot and counterplot that had led to this day.

The door wasn't locked. She flung it open and ran inside.

And stopped.

Here was the monstrous stone fireplace with the mocking crest of Oakhurst above it—the oak tree with the serpent coiled among its branches, the reversed Cup and the broken Sword, and above them the Bear, Arthur's symbol, slain, its head set upon a silver plate. Mordred had blazoned his intentions in plain sight, knowing none of his enemies would possess the memories that would let them read it.

Here was the grand double staircase that led to the upper floors, its carpet sodden with water and white with mildew.

But the great Tree that should have stood between the staircases was gone.

"*No!*" she screamed. "Where is it?"

"Gone." Burke had followed her in.

"They moved it. We're too late." Loch came forward and knelt upon the tile floor. He reached out and brushed away dirt and leaves to reveal a thin band of metal and the sheared-off remains of several metal spikes. "They must have taken it out just after the fire." He stood, and pointed up toward the ceiling. "You can see where it was. And look—there are marks all over the floor. They probably dragged it out on some kind of sled."

"And now it is secure within the walls of their great fortress," Dagonet said, joining them. "And the day is lost."

"No," Spirit said suddenly. "No, wait. It isn't."

She turned around. Most of the "army" had followed her

inside. A couple of them had even ridden their horses up the steps. "We can still win!" she shouted.

"How?" Angelina shouted back. "Because it sure looks like that tree is gone."

"Yes!" Spirit said. "They took it—and it's at The Fortress now. Mordred didn't dare leave it unprotected! He walks this world again, just as he swore he would—but it is his own necromancy that allows it, not The Merlin's magic. And so, I see a path to victory. You, Dagonet, and you, Loholt, and you, Gareth—all of you belong to this time and place. So do I. But Mordred doesn't. He is not a Reincarnate, like the Grail Knights or the Shadow Knights. He has stepped from the world in which he was imprisoned to this one."

"And I am sure you're about to tell us how that means we haven't just lost," Gareth said, sounding in that moment more like Dylan Williams than he did like a Grail Knight of Arthur's Court.

"It means he's expecting another battle like Camlann," she answered instantly. "Why not? It was his big defeat—but this time, he thinks he can't lose. He knows by now he'll be facing the Grail Knights, but why should he worry? We're a bunch of teenagers. He's got us outnumbered. He's got the Shadow Knights. He's got The Fortress. And—don't forget—he's got hostages." Everyone in his brand new peasant village was an innocent bystander, and Spirit was sure Mordred wouldn't hesitate to kill them if that would bring him triumph.

"You are not making a really convincing case for our victory," Burke said in a low voice.

"So if he wants Camlann Part Two—we're going to pretend to give it to him," Spirit said. "We're going to feed him the Middle Ages until he chokes on it."

"'On second thought, let's not go to Camelot! It is a silly place!'" Kelly called from the back of the crowd.

For an instant Spirit froze in disappointment. Then she recognized the quote—*Monty Python and the Holy Grail*—about the same time everyone else did.

Burke and Loch began to whoop with laughter. And Spirit joined them.

Mark Rider had had better days.

Twenty years ago, on the eve of his graduation from Oakhurst, the man he'd known as Dr. Vortigern Ambrosius, Headmaster of Oakhurst Academy, had summoned him to his office. And there, Mark's entire world had been turned inside out. He'd been given the chance to live, to serve Mordred of Britain as his Shadow Knight—or to die, his magic blasted from his mind.

It hadn't been a hard choice to make.

Not then.

For more than twenty years he'd enjoyed the wealth and power that came of being a member of Mordred's Inner Circle. In his other life, he'd been a king. In this life, he had a kingdom his other self couldn't have imagined—a business empire that brought him millions of dollars, and international adulation. He had a queen as his wife—Morgause of Orkney.

Even Tristan had been returned to him—his brother Teddy. None of them could imagine a better life than the one they had—using their magic, secretly, on all the mundane cattle of the world. There had been nothing beyond their reach. And the Shadow Knights had gathered around Breakthrough's banner. It was Mordred's long-forgotten battle-standard. A fine joke, Mark had thought once.

He'd known his master meant to rule. It was why Breakthrough had been created, and why the shadow-network of corporations controlled by Breakthrough had been built. Money was power. In this new world, one didn't need noble birth or great armies—only money. And so Mark had thought he knew what Mordred meant to do. Between money and magic, he could make himself President of the United States of America. Bend the government to his will as he could so easily do, and he could make Great Britain a colony. He would rule over an empire vaster than any they'd once known. He could make himself, with time and patience, ruler of all of Earth.

And then Mark had discovered what Mordred's true plans were. Not to rule Earth as it was—but to smash it into a caricature of ancient Britain, the kingdom he had lost, and rule over that.

And Mark couldn't stop him.

He'd tried. When Mordred first summoned him to tell him the time was near, and to tell Mark what part he would play, he'd protested. Tried to argue for a more modern endgame. But no one who wished to live would willingly face the

Black Dragon's fury. And so Mordred had given his orders. And Mark had obeyed them.

Even Tristan and Morgause think this is a good idea, he thought bitterly. *Tristan has never thought past his next entertainment, and my beloved wife thinks she can trade a queen's crown for an empress's coronet.*

Morgause meant to betray him the moment she no longer needed him. Tristan thought gleefully of a world in which there was no law but his own whim. Mark was the only one who thought Mordred's plan was madness, and he kept his mouth shut. If any others among the Shadow Knights feared what was to come, they kept their thoughts well hidden. Even when the plan moved to its final stages—gathering the locals together and englamouring them—Mark heard no whisper of complaint from his people. Why should he? They were going to be the new rulers. The Shadow Knights had gathered from across the globe, converging on this insignificant little town in the middle of nowhere to wait for the moment of Mordred's triumph.

Mark climbed the stone steps that led to the ramparts of The Fortress. The morning breeze ruffled his hair. It was a beautiful spring day. From here he could see the highway. Cars sped by, filled with motorists who had no idea the world was going to end a fortnight from today. He could feel the thrum of magic beneath his feet as Breakthrough's Jaunting Mages emptied warehouses a hundred miles distant, filling the storerooms of The Fortress with the last of the necessary supplies. Below him, he could see peasants tilling the fields. There was no need for that: an Earth Mage could cause a crop to spring up, ripe and ready for harvest, with nothing more than a spell. But Mordred's world had contained peasants, and so peasants he must have.

You think ill of your liege at your peril, Mark of Cornwall, he reminded himself. *Mordred sees and knows all. And yet. . . .*

And yet Prince Mordred had not seen enough to know those five children plotted against him. Even Morgaine, who he'd been so certain was already theirs, had defied him. And Agravaine had slain her. But the other four had escaped. Worse, they'd returned bearing the Hallows of Britain, to free the rest of the young mages held prisoner at Oakhurst— children for whom Mordred had plans that did not involve their survival.

Mark had ordered the rebels found and recaptured, of course. He'd thought it would be safe, for he'd ordered that none of them be harmed, only captured. But Mordred had been furious that he'd given any order at all, and forced him to call his knights back—nor had Mark dared to refuse.

But he knew it was a mistake.

If they have the Hallows, they know who they are now. When next they meet, Mordred will not face frightened children, but Knights of the Grail. Why does he not see his peril?

Perhaps, Mark thought, *what Mordred sees is a chance to flaunt his final victory before his greatest enemies. But that is madness.*

Perhaps—

Suddenly a gleam of light caught his eye. There, to the west, there was movement. Horses, coming from the direction of Oakhurst.

Suddenly, in the distance, he heard the mellow call of horns. He turned to the nearest sentry. "There is nothing to see here," he said meaningfully. "I am going to my chambers."

✦

L och carried the banner. It wasn't much of a banner, but then, they weren't much of an army. They'd scavenged what they needed from the theater and the music room: a blue sheet with a hastily-painted-on white horse, stapled to a yardstick that was nailed to a pole. Renee and Peredur rode behind him. They'd been in the orchestra, and their French Horns had still been in the music room. When they reached the place where the edge of the town had been, they stopped and sounded the call to battle. The notes were loud in the stillness.

Then they rode on.

✦

W hat's going on?" Brenda demanded nervously from the back of the black van.

"Did I know, be certain I would say," Addie answered irritably.

Something had gone wrong. She knew it.

She'd waited with Veronica and Brenda (trying not to think of them as "the mortalfolk," trying to remember she was Adelaide Lake, not Vivianne of Avalon) while the others rode out. Her Hallow was perhaps the most powerful of the Four—the Cauldron of Plenty, which could provide anything its possessor asked of it. The Cauldron had made Avalon a center of healing and peace . . .

. . . and those memories, of a lifetime spent coolly ruling over the lives and fortunes of all who came to her for help, were not what Addie wanted for herself. She wanted to *matter*. She wanted to make a difference.

She wasn't sure, any more, where Addie Lake ended and Vivianne began.

All I know is, powerful or not, it's a very awkward Hallow to wield, if what you want to do is follow your friends into trouble.

"We're not just going to sit here, are we?" Veronica said.

The black van—the Cauldron of Plenty—was parked behind a stand of trees directly opposite the gates of The Fortress. Addie couldn't remember what had been here when Radial had still existed. Maybe nothing.

"There's nothing else we can do," she said. "The fog is gone. If I move, we'll be spotted. We have to wait for the others to get back."

"Well, I'm not waiting!" Veronica said. Before Addie could stop her, she shoved open the side door of the van and jumped out.

"*Veronica!*" Addie cried.

"There's got to be something!" Veronica called back over her shoulder. She started running toward the village.

"Sorry, sorry, sorry," Brenda said, opening the passenger door. "I'm sorry—we have to!" She followed Veronica.

Addie pounded on the steering wheel in frustration.

Then she heard the sound of the horns.

I can't just sit here either, she thought, and turned the key in the ignition.

The van rolled forward.

※

Mordred's knights had made a wide trampled path leading from The Fortress around the southern edge of the village. They followed it. Every few minutes, Peredur and Renee blew their horns.

"Shouldn't they have come out by now?" Burke asked in a low voice.

"They should," Spirit agreed uneasily. "We're giving Mordred exactly what he wants. We're riding to battle as if we're living in medieval Britain."

"So where are the legions of hell?" Burke asked.

Spirit had no answer, then: "Look," she said, pointing.

The walls of The Fortress were filled with people watching them advance. Hundreds of them, all in the red-and-black of Breakthrough.

And of Mordred.

※

There was no way Mark could keep it a secret that the missing Oakhurst students had turned up and apparently gone mad. They couldn't possibly be riding to The Fortress to surrender—not if they rode beneath the White Horse banner. But he'd learned his lesson well: Mordred did not summon him, and so Mark did not summon his Shadow Knights to ride into battle.

By now, nearly everyone—everyone human, that was—from The Fortress was on its walls. The top of the wall was twenty feet wide. There was room for everyone. Shadow Knights, Gatekeepers—everyone who served Mordred was here. Waiting.

"We aren't just going to watch, are we?" Tristan asked. "I could—"

Mark grabbed his arm before Tristan could prepare a spell. "You could join the others our liege lord has sacrificed to feed his great spell, if you defy him," he snapped. "Let them come."

"Surely Prince Mordred has power enough to destroy them without our help," Morgause said silkily. Her bright hair whipped around her face in the morning as she leaned out over the parapet. "We must allow him the glory of that victory."

"Yes," Mark said meaningfully. "We must indeed."

*

The black van was waiting for them at the gates of The Fortress. The building's gates stood open. There was as much space between them as a four-lane highway. This time, when Peredur and Renee sounded the call to battle, the sound echoed back off the stone walls, as if the horns had been blown inside a giant parking garage.

The column of riders walked their horses forward. The van gunned its engine and rolled along beside them.

This was the first time Spirit had actually seen inside the walls of The Fortress. She didn't think anybody outside of Breakthrough actually had. It might have been a little hard to explain. There was an open courtyard the size of a football field. It was grass, not stone, just as the inner courtyard of a castle would have been centuries ago. At the far end was Mordred's keep. There was really no other word for it. Like the walls, the building itself was grey granite. Steps the width of the entire building went up to the main entrance. The stairs gave onto a deep portico. The entrance itself was set back. It was high enough above the ground that there was probably a full floor below it, but if there was, it had no windows. The floors above overhung it, so its doors—and whatever decoration they had—were lost in shadow. But above the entrance the Breakthrough logo was displayed, a shield in carved relief, three stories tall.

No. It's not the Breakthrough logo. It never was. It's Mordred's symbol.

At the foot of the granite steps stood the thirty-foot-high trunk of the Gallows Oak. For a moment, Spirit wondered why it was out here, instead of locked up in a vault somewhere. Then she saw that the ground around it was muddy and dark, and she understood.

Blood sacrifices. Mordred's a necromancer. He's been making sacrifices to renew his body and let it out of the Tree. But the people he's killed haven't given him enough power to do that. He needs to sacrifice magicians.

He needs to sacrifice us.

The top of the walls around the courtyard were deserted now.

"Yoo-hoo?" Loch called. "Anybody home?" His voice rang off

the stone walls. Silence greeted his words. "Okay, we do it your way," she heard him mutter. He cleared his throat. "I, Lancelot du Lac, King in my own land and vassal of Arthur of Britain—"

Suddenly the temperature in the courtyard seemed to drop. In the shadows of the portico, Spirit saw movement.

It was Mordred.

He wasn't pretending to be Oakhurst's eccentric headmaster any longer. He wore a long black robe of some fabric that ate light. Symbols embroidered in dull silver thread covered the arms and the chest, gleaming sullenly as the sunlight struck them. On his head he wore a diadem of blackened silver set with rubies the size of hen's eggs.

And behind him the shadows filled as his army came to join him. None of them were Shadow Knights. None of them were even human. There were giants in ragged wolfskins, their bodies grey with dust. Tall gaunt pale creatures with glowing red eyes who stood cloaked in their own leathery wings. Creatures that looked like gigantic rats—they walked upright, and beneath their patchy fur, their skin was yellowed and sickly. Trolls with wide flat faces, their mouths gigantic and filled with gleaming shark-teeth. Things that looked like dead trees—if trees could walk, and had eyes. Among them slunk creatures that looked half like wolves, and half like weasels, with black beady eyes and long narrow snouts.

They were all the nightmares anyone had ever had, all the creatures half-glimpsed in the paintings at Oakhurst's last dance. They belonged in some Halloween night, not in the sunlight of an April morning.

At Burke's side, Cafall barked once, and was silent.

"So, Arthur, we meet again," Mordred said. He walked slowly down the steps. "Have you come to beg for your life? Perhaps I will spare your people if you do. Did you imagine, even when you lay dying, that we would meet again? Only this time, it is to celebrate my victory. Gaze upon your pitiful army and despair! You cannot hope to defeat me, for at last, after centuries, my triumph—"

"No."

Spirit urged Passelande forward, past Burke, past Loch.

"You aren't fighting him," she said. "You're fighting me."

Gripping Excalibur in one hand and Passelande's mane in the other, she slipped from the horse's back and walked forward.

"Your fight has always been with me."

For one moment, there was absolute silence. Mordred stared at her as if he had not understood the words that had come from her mouth. As if she had spoken a foreign tongue. Then, in an instant, the blank expression turned to apoplectic and absolute fury.

"You puling nonentity!" Mordred shrieked. His face was scarlet, nearly purple, with disbelief and rage. "How dare you! You nothing—you wife—you *girl!*"

Girls rule, boys drool, Muirin's voice seemed to sing-song mockingly in Spirit's mind. Spirit was too smart to say that aloud.

And anyway, before she could have, Mordred attacked.

❧

NINE

Black fire boiled out of Mordred's hand. Automatically Spirit swung Excalibur up to parry. The fire turned red, then orange, as it sprayed off the blade. *Didn't know you'd be training your enemies when you made us take all that swordfighting, did you?* she thought.

Behind Mordred, his army of nightmare horrors raced down the steps to join the fight. She heard scattered screams from behind her as the others caught sight of what they were facing. *You were right, Arthur. If I had not wakened the Grail Knights, this would have been over before it began.* But with the Grail Knights among them, eager for battle, the magicians of Oakhurst not only stood their ground—they fought back.

She saw one of the tree-things go up in a rush of flame. It howled as it burned, a low sound like timbers creaking. One of the bat things rose into the sky, only to be smashed to the ground by a blast of wind. Gareth—the Kitchen Knight, they'd once called him—had brought a backpack filled with all the cutlery he could find in the cafeteria—he flung knives, forks, spoons into the air, and Jaunted them with lethal accuracy at his targets.

But she had little attention to spare from her own battle. Mordred was screaming in fury, lashing out at her with attacks she could see, and attacks she could only sense. Each time she deflected a spell with her blade she felt it ring, as if Excalibur, too, was challenging their great enemy.

Burke fought at her right side, and Loch at her left. Burke's fists—the Shield—glowed with a radiance matched only by Loch's Spear. She saw Burke pound one of the attacking giants, and then fling it aside using a move she recognized from *Systema*. On the left, she saw Cafall spring up to savage one of the wolf-weasels, leaping away again as Loch finished it with the Spear. Each time one of the Hallows struck its target there was a blinding flash, and the monstrous creature vanished.

If her army had not been outmatched a hundred to one, it would have been an easy victory. Her allies had spread into a ragged line. Some of her warriors were still mounted, but anyone who didn't have one of the Air Gifts fought afoot, for their horses would not approach the enemy.

On the walls above them, the Shadow Knights gathered once more.

On the ground below, the Grail Knights and their allies fought.

Mordred had conjured a sword out of nothingness. It was

black from point to hilt, and its surface rippled and shimmered as if it were on fire. Each time Spirit's blade clashed with his, there was a screeching sound loud enough to be heard over the roar of combat.

And slowly, step by step, she gained ground.

Mordred was not her true target.

Excalibur breaks all magic, Guinevere whispered in her mind.

It was the thing that might save them—and the world. All the Reincarnates, all the Mages, *had* magic. But Mordred *was* magic. He held his stolen body only by virtue of his sorcery. Destroy that—and he was nothing. He knew—he *had* to—that she'd tried twice to destroy the Gallows Oak. In his frenzy to defeat her, he thought she'd changed her target.

But she hadn't.

Step by step she fought him back across the field. The ground beneath her feet was mud now, slippery and treacherous, sodden with water and ichor and blood. As she spun to block an attack from one of the trolls, she caught a glimpse of the black van. Its back doors were open, and Addie was dragging one of the Oakhurst students into it. *Mobile Alchemy Sorcery Hospital,* Spirit thought whimsically, then the moment was gone as she gathered herself against Mordred's new onslaught.

He should have defended the Tree, but she could see that instead he was slowly turning his forces to flank her fighters. He meant to reach the gates and bar them, trapping the Grail Knights and their allies inside his fortress walls so he could slaughter them at his leisure. He didn't realize that every one of his attackers knew it didn't matter whether they were locked in or not. They had to win. Here. Now.

Another step, and another. Her arms ached with weariness. Her legs were leaden. This was worse than the most hellish Endurance Ride, the longest *Systema* class. She didn't know how long she'd been fighting all out, but she was tiring.

She heard Loch scream. One of the bat-things had dived on him from above. She saw its claws shred through the armor he wore as if it were tissue paper. Cafall leaped, jaws wide, tearing at the foe. There were trolls running toward Loch, but he couldn't see them.

"Burke!" she shouted, and Burke turned to attack them.

And Mordred struck.

The ground boiled beneath her feet as if an earthquake had hit, and suddenly, tearing loose from the mud came vines, each one covered with long needle-sharp thorns. She hacked at them desperately, knowing she was dead if any of them coiled around her. But she could not defend against the vines and Mordred's blade at the same time.

She saw the descending blow, and flung Excalibur up to block it, but she was too slow. It struck her shoulder as she desperately flinched away. The steel shoulder-guard she wore crumpled like a Coke can; she felt a burning coldness as the blade bit into flesh. Spirit stumbled aside, barely able to dodge the worst of it, and tripped, staggered, fell.

Into the thorn-vines.

For an instant they began to tighten around her.

Then they shattered, grey with ice.

She didn't pause to bless her good fortune, or to see whose spell had destroyed them. She scrabbled to her feet, using Excalibur as a crutch, and staggered forward. For a few precious seconds, no one was attacking her. Mordred had seen her fall and thought she was finished. He'd turned to Burke, wanting the battle he'd expected.

Mordred against Arthur for the fate of the world.

Her left arm was useless now. Her shoulder was numb where Mordred's baneblade had struck her, and the cut on her arm was gushing blood. Clutching her sword in her right hand, Spirit staggered toward the Tree. Behind her, she heard Burke shout a warning. Mordred had seen her.

She gritted her teeth against the pain, raised her sword in her free hand, and struck the Gallows Oak with all her strength. The blade bit into the wood, and Spirit felt the upwelling of her magic, everyone's magic—the power of her knights, her friends, everyone here today who fought in the service of the Grail—roaring through her body and down the blade like a torrent from a fire hose.

The tree . . . exploded. Its golden wood turned grey and soft, rotting away before her eyes. Day turned to night. An icy wind rose up, wailing, turning the mud beneath her feet to ice. Silence spread like the ripples in a pond, as all across the battlefield, the fighting just . . . stopped. The trunk cracked, then split, its shards and splinters whipped away in the wintery gale, falling to pieces as if it had been struck by invisible lightning. At its heart she caught a glimpse of blackened bones wrapped in ancient chains, and a hideous stench, foul even in the icy wind, filled the air. As she stared, the bones began to crumble.

Turn and fight, you fool! Mordred attacks!

Spirit hauled her blade out of the trunk, and turned.

The battlefield was silvery, as if it was midnight under a full moon. Mordred leaped toward her, his face distorted in a scream of elemental rage. As the skeleton chained in the Tree rotted away, she saw his body suddenly spurt blood from a dozen bullet holes. And suddenly, she heard Stephen Wolferman's voice, as clearly as if he were here beside her.

"The night of the big storm there was bad voodoo going down. We all knew it. The aliens had followed us. And one of them shot Roadhog, and that opened the gate, and Kenny said run, and there was blood everywhere and the shadows came out of the blood. . . ."

The night the Hellriders accidentally freed Mordred from his prison, he'd possessed the body of Kenny Hawking. But Kenny had been shot that night. For all these years, Mordred had used his power to hold Death at bay.

But now his power was failing.

And Kenny Hawking was dying. At last.

She saw Mordred fall to his knees, his face twisted with hatred and rage. With his last ounce of strength, he struck at her. She felt as if an icy spear had transfixed her, taking with it the last of her strength.

And Spirit fell.

Addie wasn't sorry not to be in the thick of the battle. She was busy enough. Their side, outnumbered as it was, was fighting with all of its strength and skill. Fires roared and flared, thunder cracked as storm winds were conjured out of nothingness, jets of water spurted up out of the ground to become spears of ice. The battlefield was a haze of spells. The Illusion Mages conjured up an entire army of armored knights to confuse the enemy, but illusions were only that: shadows, unable to strike. Their army was badly outnumbered.

Cei was the first to fall. She saw him go down beneath the clubs of two of the Stone Giants, and almost before they turned away, she was running out onto the field. With strength she hadn't known she possessed, Addie grabbed him beneath the arms and dragged him toward safety.

Toward the Cauldron.

He was still alive, barely. His face was a mask of blood, and he had too many broken bones to count. He screamed, once, as she hauled him upright and shoved him into the back of the black van.

Heal! she commanded.

The uprush of Power from this, the most powerful of Britain's Hallows, made her step back in surprise. But before it had done its work, she had turned back to the field, looking for more of the fallen.

She did not see the battle itself. It was not her concern. It had moved toward the steps, leaving behind it the injured and the fallen, and they were what she saw, for she was the Lady of

Avalon, in whose Gift lay all the healing arts, and mastery of the Cauldron. Again and again she made the painful journey across the field to gather up another body to place inside the Cauldron. There were so many. She could not save them all.

"Let me help."

She looked up, startled. Veronica was there, with Brenda, with a dozen other kids whose names she didn't know. There was no time to ask why Brenda and Veronica had come back, or why the others had come at all. "Bring them!" she said, and she and Veronica dragged Angelina Swanson back to the van.

Each time she felt the golden tide of inexhaustible magic rise up, and each time it receded, another Grail Knight or Oakhurst Mage staggered out, alive and healed, to grab weapons and return to the fight. She didn't know how long it went on. Once, it was Veronica Davenport they manhandled into the Cauldron. She'd been struck down as she dragged a fallen fighter from the field.

Then the sun went black.

✦

Mark stood on the battlements watching the battle below. It disturbed him that Mordred had not summoned the Shadow Knights to battle. The army he had chosen to lead against Arthur and his pitiful band of children was drawn from the legions of Otherrealm.

It would have been madness to set the sprites and spirits of Otherrealm against the Grail Knights, were Mordred not able to call forth such overwhelming numbers. Again and again, Mark saw trolls, lamiae, Waldgeists, Stone Giants struck down by a single blow from one of the Hallows of Britain.

But for each creature slain, there were a dozen to take its place.

"Come on!" Tristan tugged at his sleeve. "We're going to miss all the fun!"

"The slaughter, you mean." Mark of Cornwall had spent most of his previous life fighting—like any other knight, he thought of warfare as not only his duty, but as his pleasure. But war had rules. Half of Arthur's force was nothing more than children.

"War, slaughter, who cares as long as we win?" Tristan said impatiently.

"When my liege summons me to battle, then I will go," Mark said imperturbably. He turned to face Tristan. "And you'd better not stick your nose in where you aren't invited either. The last time we overstepped Prince Mordred's orders, the results were . . . unpleasant."

Even Tristan winced at that. Mordred had struck dead the messenger who came to tell him Mark was hunting the escaped Oakhurst students.

"But how could he object to our loyalty?" Morgause purred, twining her arm through Mark's. "We are his sworn vassals. What greater joy could there be than to support him on the field of battle?"

Even Mark had to admit Morgause was lovely. Her cheeks

were flushed with excitement, and her eyes sparkled. She was a woman any man would prize . . .

. . . if only he could trust her not to knife him as he slept.

"'Greater joy?'" he asked. "Surviving his anger would be high on my list." He turned away, gazing out at the carnage below. He heard the screams of children, the shouts of the Grail Knights—and the inhuman baying of the monsters Mordred had set upon them.

When he next looked away from the battle, Tristan and Morgause were gone. They weren't the only ones, either.

Sudden alarm filled him. It wasn't like either of those two to leave the scene of a battle. If they couldn't fight themselves, the next best thing was to watch.

And better than either is the chance to betray an ally—and to indulge themselves at the same time.

He knew Morgause blamed Spirit White and the others for the death of Morgaine. She'd been so sure Muirin Shae would join them. She'd lavished favors and privileges on the girl—not out of love, Mark knew perfectly well, but from arrogance. Morgause enjoyed wielding power—and what greater power could she have over her Reincarnate sister than to be the one who had been responsible for bringing her into the Shadow Knights?

But Morgause had been cheated of that victory, and now she thought she was going to be cheated of the chance to kill those responsible with her own hands.

But if she took the field and claimed it was by his orders,

Morgause would have the sweets of self-indulgence—and it would be Mark who would face the bitter punishment.

Snarling, he ran for the stairs.

✦

Mark caught up to her just as Morgause was leaving her rooms. She'd taken time to armor herself and put on her sword.

"Stop," he said. "I have not given you leave to join the battle."

She pushed up her visor and smiled. "Dear Mark. Always the soul of chivalry when it's most inconvenient. Do you think I give a damn what you permit and what you don't?"

Before she'd finished speaking, she lashed out at him with her sword. Mark dodged back out of reach. His Gift, like his brother's, was from the School of Fire. It wasn't terribly useful against a sword.

But a gun was.

He drew it as Morgause came for him again. She laughed as she saw the pistol, and raised her sword.

She didn't laugh as he fired. The bullets in the clip were Black Talon armor-piercing rounds. They could penetrate modern tactical armor as if it were a feather pillow. Armored in chain mail, Morgause had no chance.

She fell to the floor, dying. He kicked the sword away from her hand. She was trying to draw the dagger at her belt, but she was too badly wounded.

"You always placed too much trust in the Middle Ages, Morgause," he said.

"Tristan . . . will avenge. . . ." she whispered as she died.

And that raises the interesting question of where Tristan is, if not with you, my late treacherous lady. He knew Tristan wasn't already on the field. Mark had moved too fast for that.

I have to find him.

Fire was not a School that lent itself to spells of seeking and finding, but Mark and Tristan shared one thing that few of the Oakhurst alumni could claim: they really *were* brothers. It was one of the few times that two children in a family had both been born with magic—and so Mordred had spared both of them when he slew their parents. The ties of blood kinship would let Mark find Tristan no matter where he was. He stepped back from the spreading pool of blood on the floor, closed his eyes and concentrated. A moment later, he could see through Tristan's eyes.

And what he saw chilled him with horror.

Mark paused only to snatch up Morgause's sword from the floor, and ran.

❋

Are you sure this is what Doctor Ambrosius wants me to do, Teddy?" Clark Howard asked nervously.

He'd been down in the Game Room when Teddy came looking for him—he knew there was some kind of student uprising going on among the kids who'd run away from the school, and he really didn't want to be involved. Much better if he could visit them in the dungeon later and present himself as a nice guy who could get them out of trouble for a little friendly cooperation.

He knew about the Master Plan, and that Doctor Ambrosius was the real brains behind all of Breakthrough. They'd finished the last hack three days ago, in plenty of time for Doc A's schedule. He wanted to launch on May First, because that was a big holiday in the old Soviet Union, and it would help convince everyone that the Russians were behind this. Clark thought that was pretty neat: not only would Breakthrough be the only ones with magic after the missiles flew, they'd be the only ones with much of *anything*. The whole world would become one giant amusement park owned by Breakthrough. And he'd be able to do anything he wanted.

"Would I be here now if he didn't?" Teddy asked, smiling. "You can do it by yourself, can't you?"

"Of course I can," Clark said, irritated. "I wrote most of this code. All I need to do is get into the server and send it." Teddy was just like his brother Mark: a rich prettyboy executive who never got his hands dirty. Unlike people like Clark, who actually had useful job skills and had to work for a living. *Not as soon as this goes live,* he told himself gleefully. *Once the Black Dragon rises for real, it'll be just like the game, for everyone. . . .*

"Okay," Teddy said, smiling. "Party on, dude."

Clark ignored him, opening the browser window and beginning to type. There were piles of printouts and manuals surrounding his workstation, but he didn't need them any more. Like he'd said, he'd written the code. And it was just waiting in the library to upload.

"*Stop!*"

Clark jumped at the sound of Mark's voice. He took his hands off the keyboard.

"What are you doing?"

"It's called a first strike, dear brother," Teddy said. "Why wait? The element of surprise is crucial in war. You've told me that often enough."

"You idiot," Mark snarled, striding toward him. "You'll kill us all!"

"Keep typing," Teddy said, in a low voice. He turned and walked toward Mark, drawing his sword as he went.

Clark actually thought the swords were the best part of this whole deal. Swords were cool. When Mark had moved them all to Nowhere, Montana, all of them had gotten swords. Armor, too, just like in *Rise of the Black Dragon*. He didn't like that as much, because it was a lot heavier than it looked, but the sword was awesome. Some of the guys (like Teddy) went overboard on the whole medieval Dark Knight thing, wearing their swords and armor most of the time. Clark preferred to be comfortable.

He winced at the first sound of sword on sword. Mark and Teddy were really going at it. He turned away from his console to watch.

"Hey, guys?" Clark called after a moment. "You want to take it outside?" If any of the equipment got damaged, Doc A was going to flay everyone involved. Or even anyone nearby.

Both men ignored him.

Clark got nervously to his feet. Maybe it would be a good idea if he got out of here, and made like he'd never been here at all. The only problem was, there was only one entrance to the computer room, and Mark and Teddy were fighting right in front of it. He edged nervously along the wall. Maybe they'd move further into the room and he could make a run for it.

He'd never realized that swordfighting could be so *loud*.

At least they aren't using magic, he thought hopefully. *The last thing we need down here is a fire.* . . .

As if his thoughts had been a spell of Summoning, there was a wash of flame. Every scrap of paper in the computer room caught fire at once in a choking wave of heat. Over the crackling of the flames, Clark saw Teddy fall to the ground.

He killed him! Mark killed him!

He heard the fire alarm begin to sound, and the fire suppressant system—too little, too late—began flooding the room with carbon dioxide. The fire-door rolled down over the entrance, and as it did, Mark stepped back into the hall.

Clark screamed and ran toward the door. "Hey! Wait! Don't! You can't shut the door! *I'm still in here!*"

Outside, the sun went black and the ground turned to ice, but Clark Howard wasn't aware of that.

And a few moments later, he wasn't aware of anything at all.

☙

Lancelot du Lac, King in my own land and vassal of Arthur of Britain—"

The words had come without thought. Why not? They

were true. He was as much Lancelot du Lac as he was Lachlan Galen Spears—probably even more so. He remembered being an old man with aching joints and old battle scars, tending the herb garden in the monastery at Glastonbury. That was a part of the story most people didn't know. Lancelot had taken holy orders after Mordred's defeat and lived half his life in the cloister.

Why not? Arthur was dead, and if Mordred hadn't actually won, he'd smashed Arthur and Guinevere's shining city. Camelot had been no more.

But the dream had survived, because Lachlan Spears remembered reading *The Once and Future King*, and so he knew it had, even though he'd never imagined he'd be living it. But from the moment he held the Spear of Britain in his hands, he'd known—they'd both known, Loch and Lancelot—that this moment would come.

The moment when they had to fight.

When he had to kill.

He'd kept his worries to himself. The others had been dealing with their own problems: Guinevere, Arthur, The Lady of the Lake. Each of them had a burden of memory that wasn't just some fun Past Life Memory™ that let you brag about being Cleopatra or Napoleon, but an identity that was as real, *more* real, than the ones each of them had grown up with.

This time.

From the first moment Loch had realized what they were up against, that it was only the four of them and the Hallows against Mordred and his Empire of Evil, he'd doubted they could win. It didn't matter. Not to fight would have been worse, even though Lancelot's memories gave Loch nightmares. Loch had grown up as a victim of the cruelest sort of bullying. He'd never wanted to hurt anyone.

Loch Spears had never believed there was anything worth fighting for.

He'd been wrong.

At least today he was spared the knowledge that he was killing other people. The things here within the walls of The Fortress were the stuff of nightmare, but at least they weren't human.

And at least he wouldn't have to live with himself afterward.

It was amazing how easy violence was. He'd only had a moment to catalogue the foe—trolls and hellhounds, Waldgeists and giants, lamiae and dwerro—before he was fighting for his life. The Spear spun in his hands. His enemies turned to stone, or caught on fire, or simply rotted away in seconds. It would have been a game, except for the fact he could hear the screams of the kids he was leading into battle.

With Spirit at his side, Loch fought his way forward, climbing over the bodies of monsters. Striving to reach Mordred. Sweat poured down his face, stinging his eyes. His skin burned where something not of this world had spattered him with its dying blood. And through it all, he saw Spirit fighting Mordred, shining silver blade against black, Light against Darkness.

He knew where she was going. The Gallows Oak. Mordred's one vulnerable point. And he vowed to protect her as she strove for it.

And he failed.

One of the lamiae dropped on him out of nowhere. He screamed in pain as its claws cut through his armor. Its grave-yard stench made him gag even as he fought for his life. The thing screeched, its high-pitched wail making his ears hurt, as Cafall grabbed its leg in his jaws. Then Burke was there beside him, and together they turned to face the horde of trolls that thought to take him unaware.

They were freakish, horrible things, with mottled purple skin and jaws lined with gleaming teeth. Their mouths were too huge for their faces—Loch could have stuck his head in-side easily, if he'd wanted a quick death.

They made cooing noises, like pigeons. He thought that was the worst.

The Shield of Britain flared between Loch and the trolls. His Spear could pass through it. Their weapons could not. He killed them quickly, efficiently—a thrust of his Spear into their chests or stomachs and they began to liquefy at once.

He was just turning away from the last of them as the ground shook.

Burke howled in outraged fury.

The ground was alive with twining vines, black and limber as tentacles, each covered with impossible thorns as long as his hand. Loch saw Mordred lash out at Spirit, saw the spray of bright blood as the baneblade bit flesh.

Saw her fall.

He'd thought, before this began, that when there was no more hope he'd just stop fighting. In the heat of battle, death would be quick. He knew that with her death the day was lost, but he redoubled his efforts, fighting as if he'd suddenly gone mad, stabbing at the vines, pinning them to earth, chopping at them. He heard Burke roar like the bear that was his totem, saw the flare of light as baneblade met Shield.

Then there was a wash of cold intense enough to suck the breath from his lungs. The vines shattered like glass. And impossibly, amazingly, Spirit staggered to her feet.

Her left arm hung useless at her side, but she moved grimly forward. He clambered over the brittle thorns to follow. He was just behind her as she raised Excalibur and struck the Gallows Oak.

Everyone on the field felt what happened next. It was her Gift, her Power, the power of pure Spirit, untainted by hatred or ambition, that bound all of her people together for a moment into one body, one soul, one force. It was that force that split the Tree open, exposing the true body of Mordred.

The sun went black and a storm wind rose. Blinded by the darkness, Loch staggered forward. Mordred had seen her. Mordred was attacking. His stolen body fell, dying. But from the threshold of death itself he struck at her.

Loch heard Spirit scream.

He spun, transfixing Mordred with the Spear, but it was too late. Burke ran forward. The body of Kenny Hawking, dead since 1971, dissolved into scattered crumbling bones.

The light returned.

Burke was holding Spirit in his arms.

Around them, the battlefield clattered to silence. With Mordred's death, his sorcerous allies vanished.

"Here! Burke! *Burke!*" Addie's scream cut through the silence. She was standing beside the black van at the far end of the battlefield, covered in blood. "You have to hurry!"

Loch could feel it too: like a falling tide, Mordred's death had destroyed his power and that of his followers. The power of the Grail, no longer needed, was about to vanish from the world as well. And with it, Spirit's chance for life.

Burke lifted Spirit higher in his arms and ran to meet Addie. The two of them ran down the field together, and when they reached the van, Burke flung Spirit into the back and slammed the doors.

Ouch, Loch thought. *That's gotta hurt.*

He turned and looked behind him. The once-green lawn was nothing but mud and craters now. It looked like a war zone. On it, the Army of Light stood, or sat, or knelt, clinging to their weapons. Loch began to count. When he reached twenty-six, he knew they'd won a greater victory than any they could have imagined.

Every one of them was still alive.

"We won." He tried to shout, but his voice came out a hoarse caw. The cheer they raised in answer was equally ragged, but it was followed by laughter.

And over the sound of the laughter, he heard a dull rhythmic pounding.

"Hey—hey—hey—" Loch heard Spirit shout, muffled, from inside the black van. "Is somebody going to let me out of here?"

Ten

Oddly, Spirit was never in any doubt that they'd won.

She opened her eyes, feeling as if she'd just been abruptly awakened from a deep sleep filled with strange vivid dreams. She stared up at the ceiling above her for a long dazed moment before realizing: *Oh. I'm in Vivian's van. It's the one QUERCUS left for us.* It smelled of swamp and mildew and wet dog. She wrinkled her nose as she sat up. The doors were closed, but daylight was shining in through the mud-smeared windows. She could hear noise from outside—talking, laughing, cheering—and for a moment she thought she was somehow back at Oakhurst, at one of the Saturday football games.

But she wasn't. The van was at The Fortress. Muirin was dead.

She raised a hand to her mouth, thinking of that, and then flinched away. Her hands were covered in blood. She was wearing filthy rags. A tattered sweater. Some football padding. She pulled it off, slowly.

My name is Spirit White. Today is the fourteenth of April.

She, Loch, Burke, and Addie had escaped Oakhurst three weeks ago during the Spring Fling Dance. They'd followed directions sent to Spirit by her mysterious chat-room friend QUERCUS. Only QUERCUS was really The Merlin of Britain. He'd led them to a safe haven, where they discovered they were all Reincarnates, the Grail Knights meant to oppose Mordred in the final battle. She'd been Guinevere.

Only she wasn't Guinevere now.

The Reincarnate memories that had driven her were gone. She remembered what had happened, but it was like remembering the plot of a movie she'd seen. She crawled to the door of the van and tried to open it, but it was jammed.

"Hey!" she called, banging at it. "Is somebody going to let me out of here?"

Burke opened the door in a squeal of hinges. When he saw her, his smile was radiant. "Hey," he said softly.

"Hey, yourself," she said. "I feel like I've been asleep." She looked out across the courtyard. "Wow," she said.

"'Wow,' is the word," Addie agreed. She appeared beside Burke and hugged Spirit fiercely. "We won."

"I guess. . . ." Spirit said doubtfully. "Where is everybody?"

"Well the Legions of Hell vanished along with the Gallows Oak," Loch said, walking over to them. He looked as if he had a headache. Spirit could sympathize; it looked as if all their Reincarnate memory-selves were gone, if Loch's expression was anything to go by. "But that leaves about a million Shadow Knights and Mark Rider to deal with, so. . . ."

"*Help!*"

There was movement at the top of the stairs. Spirit took a step forward. Addie did too. The rest of the kids were coming to join them, climbing through the ruts and potholes that had been a smooth lawn only a short time before. Among them were some of the Radial kids. Spirit recognized Brenda, Veronica, Adam and Tom Phillips. Even Kennedy Lewis was there.

Spirit turned back to face the steps of The Fortress as the shouting continued.

"It's Joe!" Addie said as the figure came into view.

Joe Rogers was—or should that be 'had been'?—one of the Oakhurst Student Proctors. He'd also been a member of Oakhurst's secret fraternity, the Gatekeepers. He was dressed now in what looked like a version of the Oakhurst school uniform in Breakthrough colors: black pants and blazer, red shirt, black and silver striped tie. But the tie was loose and askew, and his clothes were rumpled, as if he'd rolled down a flight of stairs in them.

"Help!" he shouted. "Somebody help! There's been an accident!"

For a moment Spirit couldn't think what to do. She hadn't liked Joe, who'd always been trying to get her in trouble, and he was one of Mordred's people besides.

"Oh, crap," Loch said. "He's going to fall." Loch ran toward the steps, sprinting up them just in time to catch Joe as he collapsed. "He's fainted!" Loch called down. "And I can see inside! There's bodies everywhere!"

"Come on!" Spirit called to the others, and followed Loch up the steps.

✳

She remembered the first time she'd seen the walls of The Fortress, and Dylan had been babbling about all the things The Fortress contained. Spirit had never figured out where he'd gotten his information, but it turned out to be right. The Fortress held dormitories, armories, gymnasiums, libraries, swimming pools—even a greenhouse. That was in addition to offices and workrooms—but there weren't as many of those as you'd expect, because The Fortress had been built as, well, a *fortress*. The main wing, where the offices were, was decorated in Early Evil Overlord—a lot of glass, a lot of black granite—and the Breakthrough logo everywhere.

I'm never going to want to play another computer game as long as I live, Spirit thought fervently.

And Loch was right. There were bodies everywhere.

"Looks like some kind of a seizure," Blake Watson said, kneeling beside a woman in Shadow Knight armor. "She's breathing, and her vital signs look good. She's just . . . unconscious."

"They're all like that," Burke said, coming in. "Well, most of them. A few of them are conscious, but disoriented. Most of them think they're in California, for some reason."

"That was where Breakthrough was headquartered until it moved here," Loch said.

"There must be hundreds of them," Spirit said.

"Hey!" Dylan came running in, skidding a little on the smooth floor. "I found the hospital. I don't think it's big enough, though," he added, looking around.

"What are we going to do?" Spirit asked dazedly. It was bad enough that every one of the Breakthrough people had apparently been struck by some kind of backlash from Mordred's death. But the townspeople had all gotten their real memories back—and the town was still gone.

"Where's the nearest working phone?" Addie demanded.

◆

It was early evening. The high walls of The Fortress cut off the last of the daylight, but in the center of the courtyard a roaring bonfire gave both heat and light. It was surrounded, whimsically, by chairs and couches looted from the offices and living quarters, and at the opposite side of the courtyard steps, there were several barbeque grills set up, with buffet tables flanking them. They held as lavish a spread as Breakthrough had ever put on back in the days when Mark had been trying to overawe Radial with his wealth and power, but Spirit thought the food tasted a lot better now.

Over the noise of the fire they could hear the roar of generators outside the walls. The Red Cross and the National Guard would probably be here by morning, but right now, the materials Breakthrough had stockpiled for the end of the world were being used to make sure everyone in Macalister County had heat, light, and a place to sleep. A tent city had been set up so nobody would have to sleep in peasant huts, and Mark had told Spirit that Breakthrough would be giving back to the town—for real, this time.

"As soon as my lawyers find out if I've got any money left," he'd added, laughing.

Mark had been one of the first Shadow Knights to recover in the aftermath of Mordred's death. Spirit's first guess had been right—with Mordred gone, so were everyone's Reincarnate selves. The new improved Mark Rider was working as hard as anyone else not only to take care of the sick and injured, but to get rid of all the evidence of Mordred's plans before the authorities showed up to ask what the hell had happened here in Macalister County. The fire in the computer center had helped, but Mark and everyone who wasn't lying in a hospital bed had spent most of the afternoon dragging out paper files and documentation to make a bonfire.

As for the few who'd died during the battle—about a dozen Breakthrough people, including Mark's wife and brother— the plan was to blame as much of that as they could on Anastus Ovcharenko. The Russian *Mafya* hitman had fled in the confusion.

And now it was time to celebrate. To give thanks for not just their victory, but for the fact they were all alive. Almost everyone was here—townspeople, Breakthrough people, and Oakhurst students. There were still a lot of missing kids (who would probably be missing forever, since Mordred had probably sacrificed them to his necromancy), but at least practically everyone Mordred had recruited to the Shadow Knights was still alive.

"I don't blame anyone," Spirit said to Burke. Both of them, like nearly everyone here, was dressed out of Breakthrough's closets, especially since none of the townspeople had really wanted to go on looking like refugees from the nearest Ren-Faire, and the Oakhurst kids had been wearing bloody rags. The two of them were sitting together on one of the couches. A few of the braver souls were up close to the fire trying to toast marshmallows, but it was a huge blaze. Nobody was having much luck.

"Neither do I," Burke said. "We were lucky. Back when we were all still at Oakhurst you broke Mordred's spell over us, so we knew what the stakes were. A lot of people weren't that lucky."

Spirit nodded silently. In one way, none of the Shadow Knights, or the Gatekeepers, or even the rank and file of Breakthrough, had gotten a real choice about what they'd done. Mordred had dazzled them with wealth and power—and dazzled them in another way, with magic.

I guess that's a thing of the past, too, Spirit thought. She remembered the moment when she'd struck at the Gallows Oak. Perhaps all of them had given their power to that blow. Or perhaps it was a byproduct of Mordred's death. All she knew was that the magic of the student Mages of Oakhurst seemed to have faded away to only a shadow of its former strength. She didn't miss her own magic—she'd only had it a short time, and never really understood it—but some of the kids were re-ally upset at losing what they'd had. The Weather Witches could predict the weather now, but not summon storms. The Fire Witches could still light a candle or a pile of tinder—but the days when they could have set the entire Fortress burning with just a single thought were over. Even the Illusion Mages could only summon up faint shadowy ghost-images now.

The Scrying Mages seemed to be the happiest of all of them about losing their Gifts.

"I guess we were all victims of Mordred," Spirit said. "And if some of us were happier than others as the minions of an Evil Overlord, well, nobody remembers much now."

"By next year, it will probably all seem like a bad dream," Burke said.

"Oh my god, I hope so," Spirit said feelingly. But Burke's comment made her wonder—where would she be in a year? She was still an orphan. So was everyone else from Oakhurst. And now, none of them had anywhere to go.

"Another one for the fire." Mark Rider walked by them, a cardboard box filled with files in his arms. He flung it high and hard, and it landed on the fire with a shower of sparks.

"What was in that?" Kelly Langley asked idly.

"Who cares?" Mark answered. "Whatever it was, it's better gone."

"How much more stuff is there to go?" Burke asked, as Mark turned away from the blaze.

"Not much," Mark answered, smiling. "Most of it's going into the furnace in the basement, then the ashes are being flushed into the new sewer system Breakthrough put in, where I defy any forensic analyst to reassemble them. But I thought you guys deserved a celebratory bonfire."

"*We* deserved," Spirit said firmly, including Mark in her words. "We all won today."

Mark bowed—an oddly courtly gesture from someone who no longer had medieval memories to draw on—and wandered off to speak to someone else.

I just hope none of the Townies completely flips out when they've had a few days to recover, Spirit thought. In the chaotic first hours after the victory, it had been Loch who came up with their cover story: a freak tornado had wiped out the entire town. It had holes in it you could drive a truck through (a really big truck), but it made a lot more sense than the truth did. *Say something enough times, and even you'll start to believe it,* she told herself.

"I finally got through to my lawyers," Loch said as he arrived to join them. "Between Spears Venture Partners Limited and Prester-Lake BioCo, we'll have enough clout to cover up everything here."

Loch was wearing a button-down shirt a few sizes too big for him under a green sweater. He sat down on the arm of the couch, and Burke put an arm around him in a quick hug.

"Oh, but there's nothing to cover up," Addie said, sitting down beside Spirit. She was holding a platter heaped with burgers in buns, and everybody took one. "It was a freak tornado. I even heard Sheriff Copeland telling Mrs. Weber that." Addie favored all of them with her best wide-eyed idiot expression.

"Oh, well, in that case. . . ." Loch said archly. Addie snick-ered.

"So . . . what do you suppose happens now?" Spirit asked. It was the question she hadn't wanted to know the answer to, but if she couldn't ask her friends, who could she ask?

"Well, first Breakthrough and Prester-Lake rebuild Radial," Loch said. "I heard Brenda Copeland say we'd all probably be wards of the County for a while—at least until all that Oakhurst stuff gets sorted out. Some of us probably have rela-tives we could be going to. I don't."

"Me, either," Addie said. "But I'm pretty sure my trustees will come swooping down and pack me off to some exclusive boarding school."

"For the rich and boring," Loch said, and Addie sighed in agreement.

"You know," Addie said hesitantly, "all the craziness, and the magic, and the making all of us fight with each other, that sucked. A lot. But friends like you guys? That really didn't."

"And Muirin," Spirit said.

"And Muirin," Addie agreed softly.

They sat in silence for a while, watching the fire. Somebody'd found a guitar somewhere, and Spirit could hear singing and playing, but by now it was too dark to see who was doing it. Spirit tilted her head back against Burke's arm. The sky was a deep blue, and the first stars had appeared.

"It's hard to believe that after all that, nothing much has really changed for us," Burke said quietly.

"Well, yeah," Loch answered. "Oakhurst may be gone—I

think Mark's planning to sneak over there and pack the sub-basements of the place with dynamite to get rid of all the stuff down there nobody ought to see—but we're all still teenaged orphans. We'll have to finish school. Somewhere."

"And someone's going to have to train new young magicians," Addie said firmly. "Weak magic is still more magic than most people have. And how do we know it won't get stronger later?"

"Do you think more people are going to be born with magic?" Spirit asked, alarmed. "Now that Mordred's dead, and the Reincarnates are all gone. . . ."

"Yeah," Loch said. "But most of the people with magic—on both sides—were just ordinary people."

"Ordinary magicians," Addie corrected.

"Ordinary magicians with a future," Burke said.

"Ah, but for an Oakhurst graduate to be merely ordinary is to *fail!*" Loch quoted pompously, and Spirit found herself laughing along with her friends.

✦

The next three weeks were a mix of boring, annoying, and ridiculous for everyone. The medieval village was dismantled and carted away, surveyors came and laid out a new town plan, Katrina cottages started appearing along the new streets as families recovered and began to rebuild. Every single government agency in existence seemed to descend on Macalister County in the wake of the "tragic disaster." That it involved about a hundred now-homeless orphans ensured that every news organization on the entire planet would show up to ask incredibly stupid questions. *"How did you feel when your parents died?"* was a real favorite, and after the first twenty or thirty times they were asked, a lot of the kids started giving snarky answers—which were taken as the flat truth, at least by *Fox News*. Fortunately, a PR firm hired by Prester-Lake BioCo showed up to manage things before any of the Oakhurst kids could get an international reputation as future socio-paths. A number of the townsfolk were happy to take in the "Oakhurst orphans"—Burke was living with the Copelands now, and Spirit was living with the Basses, who'd lost their daughter Erika to a Shadow Knight attack earlier that spring.

It was weird, Spirit thought, to get to eat pretty much what she wanted. Weird to watch television. Weird to listen to whatever music she liked. Weird to wear jeans, and wear colors that weren't cream, gold, and brown. Weird to sleep in a bedroom that wasn't pink all over.

I guess I've got a lot of things to get used to all over again, Spirit thought. *At least Burke and I aren't being split up.* But she was going to miss her other friends when they left. Now that she was out of the creepy hothouse atmosphere of Oakhurst, living in a regular house with normal people for the first time since her parents had died, it was as if losing Mom and Dad and Fee was new all over again. She liked the Basses—and Erika's younger brother, Damien—but their presence only seemed to make her loss fresh and real.

Nearly all of the Breakthrough employees, except Mark Rider, were gone by the end of the first week.

With The Fortress as one of the two buildings left standing within a hundred miles—the other one being Macalister High School, since Oakhurst had suffered a tragic and mysterious explosion the day after the tornado hit town—The Fortress quickly became the command center for all the rebuilding efforts. Mark Rider announced that he was donating the building as the new Macalister County Seat, something that Radial's Mayor Gonzales called "a humbling act of generosity."

The Oakhurst kids knew better. Mark wanted to ditch everything related to Doctor Vortigern Ambrosius, "progressive European educator and philanthropist," as much as *they* wanted to forget being student mages.

While it would be years before the county recovered from the bizarre and shattering blow it had been dealt, at least there was no shortage of money to rebuild. Loch and Addie hadn't been the only "trust fund elite" at the school. But for just that reason, the "Oakhurst family" was breaking up. As lawyers and banks and trusts were slowly contacted, the kids with someplace else to go went there. Addie and Loch had stayed, stubbornly insisting they wanted to be here for the rebuilding, but both of them were minors, and it was only a matter of time.

And finally, one day, it was time.

I can't believe I'm leaving this place," Addie said. "Alive, I mean."

"What, you call this living?" Loch wisecracked. "I'll write, you know. To all of you."

"And we'll write back," Burke said. "Come on." He started his horse forward at a gentle walk, and the others followed.

It was the first of May. Beltane. The day on which the world had been scheduled to end, only it hadn't, and only a few people—*now*—remembered it had been supposed to. Later today Loch and Addie would be driven to Billings—in an ordinary car, this time, not an Oakhurst Rolls-Royce. From there, Loch would go to a boarding school in New York State (he'd chosen it himself, and it had an aggressive anti-bullying policy, as well as a school code requiring respect for all races, creeds, and sexual orientations), while Addie was heading to Switzerland.

Because it was their last day together, Burke had organized this farewell event, and borrowed horses, too. He said they weren't going far, or going to be away long, but Mrs. Copeland had still packed a lunch that would probably have fed eight kids for two days.

They rode down Radial's new main street. It hadn't been paved yet, but the sidewalks had been poured and there was so much new construction going on that everything smelled of fresh-cut wood and sawdust. By the end of the month, there'd be actual buildings here again.

"So where are we going?" Loch asked. "Not back to Oakhurst, I hope."

"No," Burke said. "But I thought we could take a look at it for old time's sake."

"Ha," Addie said comprehensively. "You mean at the future home of the Prester-Lake School."

"I cannot believe you're naming it after yourself," Loch said.

Addie flashed him a brilliant grin. "Don't be silly, Loch. That would be vulgar. I'm naming it after my money."

"And money is never vulgar," Loch said grandly.

As a gesture of goodwill to the county (and because, Addie said, somebody had better do something with the place), a new school was going up on the grounds of what had once been Oakhurst. When it was finished, all the kids in the county would go there, but it would also have dormitory housing for any of the former Oakhurst kids who needed it. It should be ready by fall.

And someday, maybe, teenaged magicians would come here to learn to use their powers. But that time was a long way away, if it ever came at all.

"I wonder what it's going to be like going back to school," Spirit said. "To a real school, I mean."

"You'll hardly notice," Loch said. "You're going to be spending most of the time applying to colleges."

"At least *I* don't have to wonder what I'm going to take," Addie said. "Business administration. Prester-Lake is a pretty big company. Somebody's got to run it."

"Better you than me," Loch said feelingly. "I'm not sure what I want to do. Maybe become a counselor."

"Troubled teens our specialty," Burke said lightly. "Well, I'm off to medical school when I graduate. If I can find one that will have me."

"Grades are going to be a problem," Spirit said. Everyone's last year at Oakhurst had been pretty much a wash academically, not to mention the fact that all their school records had been destroyed.

"If there's one thing we all know how to do," Burke said. "It's study. The difference is, now it's going to mean something."

"Something *real*," Addie said.

They detoured around the place where the school itself had been. When they'd come to tear it down, nobody had asked why neither of the dormitory wings had windows. Now the whole area was a building site, and they couldn't just ride across it. Most of the parts of the school that had still been intact after the explosion had already been torn down, and anything that had been left had been bulldozed flat for the new construction, so the stables were gone, and the little sunken garden with the fountain, and most of the landscaping. Only the chapel and the little train station had survived from when Arthur Tyniger had put Oakhurst up in the first place

"So where are we going?" Loch asked, when they'd ridden past the train station.

"You'll see in a minute," Burke said.

The landscape ahead of them was unchanged, and unsettlingly familiar. It had been the scene of Endurance Rides too numerous and horrible to count.

And of one very important battle.

For a moment Spirit shivered in a winter wind only she could feel, thinking of the night the five of them had faced the Wild Hunt. The stand of trees where Loch had created his spelltrap—and where they'd sent the Wild Hunt's leader back to Hell—was just up ahead.

The little pine forest was, as Spirit had suspected, their destination.

"The boundary marker's still here," Loch said in surprise. He dismounted, and ran his hands over it. "The Warding's gone, though. At least I think so. It's kind of weird, not being able to tell any more."

"I think it's a good thing," Addie said. She swung down out of her saddle and took a deep breath. "*Spring!* I never realized this miserable wasteland could actually be pretty."

"A lot prettier when you aren't fighting for your life," Burke agreed with a smile. He dismounted, then reached up to haul the packs off his saddle. "I figured, since two of us are leaving and everything's changing, we should do something to mark the occasion. Not celebrate, exactly. Just mark it."

He opened the pack and pulled out, to everyone's surprise, a small foldable shovel. "We'll need this," he said.

"For what?" Addie asked. "Or do I want to know?"

"To bury this," Burke said. The next item he pulled out of the pack was a small metal canister. It had obviously been made from a short length of pipe. One end was soldered closed, and the other end had a screw-top lid.

Loch took it from him, frowning in puzzlement. "An empty hunk of pipe?"

"Not if we put stuff in it."

He stuck his hand in his pocket, and pulled out four familiar items.

A set of worn and battered keys on an old key tag with a GM logo. A tiny phone charm in the shape of an arrowhead. A white plastic ballpoint pen, its logo long since worn off. And a set of cheap pot-metal rings with designs on their faces in rhinestones: one an ace, one a diamond, tied together with a piece of string. Burke held the items out to them on the palm of his hand. Nothing but cheap trash. But need and magic had made them into more. Just as it had made them.

"Those are the Hallows," Loch said slowly. "I— In all the confusion, I never wondered what had happened to them."

"Yours was in your pocket," Burke said to Loch. "I found it when I was tossing a bunch of clothes in the wash a couple of days later. I already had the other three. The pen was in the back of the van. The keys were in the ignition. And I'd still been wearing the rings."

Addie reached out and touched the keys. "*Are* the Hallows?" she asked. "*Were* the Hallows? I'm not sure I could even tell."

"*Were*,' I think," Burke answered. "But I kind of thought . . . we might want to bury them anyway."

"Sounds good to me," Loch said. He picked up the length of pipe and held it out to Burke. "Toss 'em."

Burke tipped his hand gently, and let the four items spill into the container.

"Wait!" Spirit said, as he was about to put the top on. "There's one more thing!"

She slipped the knotted shoelaces over her head and held up the Ironkey drive.

"This was how I'd talk to QUERCUS—to Merlin," she said.

253

"Back at Oakhurst. I don't think he's out there any more, I haven't tried to use it because I didn't want to know, but. . . . I think this deserves to go in with the others."

Burke nodded. "Seems fair," he said.

Spirit dropped the Ironkey into the pipe, and Burke screwed the lid down tight. Then they all took turns with the entrenching tool, digging a small deep hole under the pine trees. When they all agreed it was deep enough, Burke placed the container at the bottom, and they filled in the hole and stomped the earth down. When the pine needles on the ground had been scattered over the place again, there was no sign anything had ever been disturbed.

"Someday, somebody's going to dig that up, you know," Addie said. "What do you suppose they'll think?"

"Just some kids playing a game," Spirit said. "You know what kids are like."

"Sure," Loch said. "Always playing around. No idea about doing something important with their lives."

Addie reached out and touched Loch's arm gently. "We already have," she said. "If none of us ever does anything else worth mentioning until the day we die, we'll have done this."

"Well I, personally, intend to do a lot of things," Spirit said firmly.

"Me too," Burke said. "Now, who wants lunch?"

ABOUT THE AUTHORS

MERCEDES LACKEY is the author of the Valdemar novels. She has collaborated with Andre Norton on the Halfblood Chronicles and with James Mallory on the bestselling Obsidian Trilogy, Enduring Flame Trilogy, and the upcoming Dragon Prophecy Trilogy. She lives with her husband in Oklahoma.

ROSEMARY EDGHILL has worked as an SF editor, a freelance book designer, a typesetter, an illustrator, and as a professional book reviewer in addition to writing numerous books. She lives in Maryland.